SNAP JUDGMENT

RICHARD T. CAHILL

BLOODHOUND
— BOOKS —

www.bloodhoundbooks.com

Print ISBN: 978-1-5040-8246-4

This book is dedicated to the memory of Donald W. Ryan, my friend and compadre.
Auf Wiedersehen, mein Freund.

CHAPTER ONE

"Son of a bitch," Larry Watson muttered, as he went over to the figure hanging from the tree, hoping silently to himself that it was a mannequin and some form of sick joke.

As he approached, the only sound was a slight creaking from the tree branch as the body swayed slowly in the breeze.

On closer inspection, it was clear to him that this was indeed a dead man. What he found surprising was how peaceful the victim appeared. In a death as brutal as hanging, one would expect to see signs of a struggle and perhaps bruises on the face or hands. At the very least, there should have been a grimace of pain and anguish frozen on the face. But this man looked like he could be asleep, except of course for the reddish-purple discoloration in the hands where some of the blood from the arms had settled, the stiffness of rigor mortis, and the fact that he was hanging from a tree branch by the neck.

Larry thought the whole scene looked more like an old painting than a murder scene. The victim appeared not to have been dead long enough for the real stench of decay to begin. Still, he made sure not to get too close. Prior experience had taught him of the various wonderful smells given off by a dead body. He had no desire to experience them again.

Larry Watson had been walking to the courthouse that crisp, late October morning when he had happened upon the body. He'd been looking forward to getting out of the cold and thinking how he had to get everything at the courthouse ready for its 8am opening.

By union rules, he had no obligation to come in early, but Larry was old school. As a matter of pride, he went through the same routine every weekday morning; up at 5:30am, out the door by 6:15am, stop by Hazel and Ed's Cafe for coffee and a donut, and arrive at the courthouse door at 6:45am.

When he reached his destination, he had turned down the main entry path that went through the meticulously maintained front lawn of the courthouse. Just at the entry to the right was the great oak tree. It had been there for centuries. Like many Rockfield residents, Larry always took a moment to admire its massive trunk and large branches that extended out over the sidewalk and to the street.

During the summer, its green leaves created a truly beautiful sight. In the early fall, the leaves turned a bright red and were even more spectacular. Today, however, was the final week of October and most of its leaves were gone. The nearly empty branches stretched out almost like a skeleton.

Larry had been gazing at those branches when he stopped suddenly, his breath catching in his throat. From one of the thick branches that extended all the way to the street was a rope. At the other end of the rope was the man swinging slightly in the breeze.

Not only was it definitely a human body, but Larry also knew who the dead man was. In fact, probably every person in Rockfield would know this man. It was Gilbert Russell.

Gilbert Russell was perhaps the most despised person in the

entire county. Just seeing his lifeless body brought back the terrible memories of the last two years. Larry remembered the panic that had engulfed Rockfield when six-year-old Jill Lawson never returned home from kindergarten.

The city had come together as almost every man, woman, and child joined with the police in conducting the largest search any of them could remember. They went through acres and acres of dense woods and even climbed two nearby peaks of the Catskill Mountains.

Reward posters featuring the adorable young face of Jill Lawson were in every business window and on every telephone pole. Media vans from Albany and New York City news networks were a regular sight. Reporters interviewed anyone willing to talk about the missing girl and her family.

Then, eight days after she went missing, police made the discovery they had been dreading. Jill's nude body was found in a shallow grave in a wooded area less than two miles from her school.

News of this find turned the people of Rockfield from concerned citizens to an angry mob seeking retribution. At every bar, restaurant, and gathering place, people loudly proclaimed the best kind of death sentence for the killer. Ideas such as burning in oil, castration, and skinning alive were heard, along with others even more barbaric.

Six months later, police made the arrest that all of Rockfield wanted. Gilbert Russell, a thirty-seven-year-old loner, was apprehended at his home. The State Police Lab determined that DNA found on the little girl's remains matched that of Gilbert; a sample taken after his conviction on a previous charge of child molestation in the State of New Hampshire.

Gilbert had only been living in Rockfield for a few months. He had kept to himself and few knew anything about him. Once his arrest photo appeared on the local news and on the *Rockfield*

Tribune's front page, he was suddenly the most infamous and despised person throughout the county.

Gilbert denied his involvement of course, but the evidence was overwhelming. In addition to the DNA evidence, police found pictures of Jill Lawson in Russell's home that proved he had been targeting and watching her for at least six weeks. Photos showed the little girl walking to and from school, as well as playing in the schoolyard and in her own backyard.

The trial went quickly. It was even more noteworthy because the District Attorney himself, J. Robert Worthington, had done the trial, something he almost never did. Court insiders like Larry Watson knew that Worthington had thoughts of running for New York State Attorney General. The current office holder had already announced his retirement and Worthington planned to ride the Russell trial all the way to the State Capitol.

The jury had convicted Russell in less than twenty minutes. Gilbert's face reddened when the verdict was read, but he refused to say anything. He just glared at his victim's parents, Al and Jamie Lawson. Mrs. Lawson buried her face in her husband's arms and cried. Al Lawson held his wife tenderly, but his eyes never left his daughter's killer. The look on the stricken father's face told everyone that he wanted to be the one to pass sentence and judgment. New York's Court of Appeals had long ago declared the state's death penalty unconstitutional, but Al Lawson clearly wanted to be the one to pull the switch or inject the needle. Who could blame him?

A few months later, Judge John J. Hardy handed down the strongest sentence permissible in New York, life in prison without possibility of parole. As he did, he told Russell that he wished he could have sentenced him to death.

Larry remembered the hushed silence in the courtroom when Judge Hardy said, "Mr. Russell, you will spend the rest of your life in prison, but if it were up to me, you would be taken from this courtroom and hanged in the town square."

A few people actually applauded at these words, including Al Lawson. For the only time in the trial, Gilbert Russell spoke. Just as the commotion from Hardy's words died down, Russell shouted, "Fuck you, asshole!"

Hardy banged the gavel for silence. Then, with a slight smile, Hardy signaled to the sheriff's deputies who had been assigned to take him to state prison and said, "Take this rat to his hole, gentlemen."

Within a couple of weeks, life moved on in Rockfield. The Russell case had been the almost exclusive topic of conversation for nearly a year, but now nobody even wanted to hear his name.

Just a week before Gilbert Russell's dead body had been discovered by Larry Watson, the case had returned to the news. The New York State Court of Appeals overturned Russell's conviction because of a significant legal error in the presentation of murder charges before the grand jury. Gilbert Russell's attorney had filed a written form advising the District Attorney's Office that Russell wished to exercise his constitutional right to testify before the grand jury.

Worthington had Russell brought to the grand jury along with his attorney, Ray Stanton. In a move of unnecessary gamesmanship, Worthington made Russell and his attorney wait for over four hours.

Eventually, Stanton became enraged and told the young assistant district attorney assigned to sit with him that he had a court appearance at 2pm and Russell's testimony before the grand jury would therefore have to be rescheduled.

In a stunning move of arrogance and stupidity, Worthington sent back a written note advising Stanton that his client either testified that day or not at all. After consulting with his client,

Stanton announced he was leaving for court, but his client would testify without the presence of his attorney. Worthington seemingly did not care and had Russell brought into the grand jury and had him testify.

Whenever a witness testifies before a New York Grand Jury, he or she automatically gets immunity unless required to issue a waiver. Defendants are always made to do that before they testify. Worthington had Russell sign the proper form.

However, the Court of Appeals ruled that Worthington's foolish actions had resulted in Russell testifying and executing his waiver without proper legal representation. The court decided that Russell's waiver of immunity was not valid. This meant that not only was the conviction vacated, but also that Russell's testimony before the grand jury gave him legal immunity. He could never be retried or held accountable for the murder of Jill Lawson.

The public reaction was one of shock and anger. For three days, the phones at the District Attorney's Office rang off the hook for hours on end. Furious residents demanded to know how this child killer had been allowed to get away with murder.

Bob Worthington was not about to take the blame for his incompetence. Instead, he called a press conference. He had all of his assistant district attorneys standing behind him as he spoke.

"It is incomprehensible to me that a monster like Gilbert Russell has been given full immunity from prosecution by this office," he said stoically, "and it makes me physically sick that tomorrow Gilbert Russell will be brought to this courthouse and ordered released from custody."

Worthington paused, withdrew a handkerchief from his lapel pocket, and dabbed at his eyes, even though nobody present could see any tears.

He cleared his throat and sniffed. "What truly breaks my

heart is that justice will be denied to little Jill Lawson and her parents," he continued.

After pausing to let his words and emotion take their intended effect, his face became tense and angry.

"Now, I must hold the party responsible for this atrocity accountable," he said.

The assistant district attorneys behind him began nervously looking at each other. They all knew that Worthington had been the one who dropped the ball. Was he resigning? The only one in the line who remained motionless was Frank Alexander, Worthington's Chief Assistant. He either knew or strongly suspected what was coming next.

Worthington suddenly turned to his left and pointed at a young man at the far end of the line. "Jason Barnes, step forward please."

Jason Barnes, the first-year prosecutor who had been assigned to sit with Russell and his attorney prior to his grand jury appearance and who had delivered Worthington's note, stepped forward and nervously asked, "Yes, sir?"

"You are the one who brought Gilbert Russell into the grand jury," Worthington charged, "and you are the one who told Attorney Stanton that he could leave. You are the reason why Gilbert Russell got immunity and the Lawson family will never get justice."

The young man's eyes widened as he realized what was happening. "What a minute," he objected, "I just did what you—"

"Silence!!" Worthington thundered, "There is no excuse for what you did. It is unacceptable. You are fired, Mr. Barnes!"

Barnes shouted in protest, as did the assembled members of the media who had all seen the decision from the Court of Appeals and knew about Worthington's note.

"Officer!" Worthington shouted, pointing at Chief

Investigator Roger Billingsley, "Remove Mr. Barnes from the courthouse."

The room went quiet as Roger Billingsley, known as Bills to his friends, stepped forward and walked over to Jason Barnes. Barnes opened his mouth to protest, but Bills cut him off.

"Come with me, son," he said compassionately, "Everything will be fine."

Tears welled in the young, now-former-assistant district attorney's eyes, as he saw his career ending almost before it started.

Bills put his hand on the young man's shoulder and said, "Trust me."

Barnes hung his head and complied. Without another word, Bills walked him out of the pressroom. Barnes was not even clear of the room when Worthington started speaking again and placed the entire blame for the matter on his former assistant.

Unbeknownst to Worthington, Bills walked Barnes right over to Judge Hardy's chambers and explained everything to an immediately irate judge. Hardy picked up the phone and called in a few favors. Before the day was out, a law firm across the river in the City of Hudson specializing in criminal defense hired Jason Barnes at quite a bit more than his prosecutor's salary. Much to Worthington's chagrin, word of this spread through the courthouse like wildfire.

The next day, Gilbert Russell was brought back to Linton County Court so he could be formally cleared and released from custody. The courtroom was standing-room-only when the sheriff's deputies brought the prisoner to the defense table. The handcuffs and shackles were removed, and the deputies walked away from the prisoner and took position near the rail that separated the audience from the court proceedings. They were obviously worried about violent reactions from those assembled.

A few minutes later, Judge Hardy entered the court and

everyone stood except Russell. He just smiled broadly and mockingly at the judge. Hardy glared at the defendant, but said nothing.

After sitting and instructing the rest of the people to do the same, he formally called the case. Turning to the prosecutor's table, he said, "Mr. Alexander, the People's position please."

Frank Alexander stood and buttoned his jacket. Bob Worthington was nowhere to be seen. He had instead assigned the matter to his chief assistant. Some speculated that he also did not want a public confrontation with Judge Hardy about Jason Barnes.

"Your Honor," Alexander said, "based on the ruling from the New York State Court of Appeals, the defendant has been granted immunity. Therefore, the charges against him must be dismissed and his unconditional release granted."

Alexander then sat down without another word. Hardy turned to the defense table. "Mr. Stanton?"

Ray Stanton stood. Known as "Toupee Ray" because of the horrible rug he always wore to hide his baldness, Stanton was clearly uncomfortable. Normally, Stanton was talkative and energetic. Today, he seemed to hate his job. He had filed the appeal that resulted in Gilbert Russell's conviction being thrown out. It had been a substantial legal victory, but Ray took no pleasure in it. He had only been doing his job, but he felt physically sick knowing this child killer was about to be set free.

"The defense concurs, Judge," he croaked before sitting.

"Very well," Hardy replied, "the defendant will please stand."

Russell did not move. He just continued to smile.

"I'm not granting your release until you stand and show respect to this court," Hardy shouted.

"Respect?" Russell asked mockingly, "You're the one who

said you wanted me to be taken to the center of town and hanged. You don't deserve any respect."

Hardy did not back down. "You either stand up," Hardy threatened, "or I will have the court officers pull you out of that chair and hold you up."

The two men glared at each other for a very long moment. Finally, Russell sneered and stood. He held out his hands and bowed to the judge in a mocking gesture. Hardy ignored the disrespectful action.

"Gilbert Russell, you were found guilty of Murder in the First Degree. The evidence shows without question that you killed Jill Lawson before she had a chance to live her life," Hardy said sternly. "Unfortunately, because of prosecutorial error, I have no choice under the ruling from this state's highest court but to dismiss all charges against you and release you."

Russell laughed aloud and said, "Can we get on with this please? I have new girlfriends to meet."

The intense shocking silence that followed Russell's repulsive comment lasted for a few seconds before the voice of Al Lawson rose from the back of the courtroom.

"You filthy animal!" Lawson shouted. "I'll kill you where you stand."

Court officers restrained Al and pleaded with him to stop fighting. Lawson's face was streaked with tears as he struggled to get free.

"That bastard killed my little girl!" he screamed helplessly.

Russell just stood there laughing as if the scene before him was the most hysterical thing he had ever seen.

Judge Hardy called for order, but his courtroom was complete chaos as people screamed and cursed at Gilbert Russell, who just kept laughing.

Eventually, two of the sheriff's deputies grabbed Russell and dragged him out of the courtroom via a side entrance. Even as he was pulled out the door, Russell never stopped laughing.

It had been two days since that despicable fiasco and now Larry Watson stood staring into Gilbert Russell's lifeless eyes. It was not until he had taken out his cell phone and dialed 911 that he noticed a note pinned to the dead man's chest. Written in fancy calligraphy, it read, "I sentence you to be hanged by the neck until you are DEAD."

TWO WEEKS LATER...

CHAPTER TWO

I landed with a loud thud. Looking up, I could see five-year-old Cindy Moore standing over me with a broad smile lighting up her face.

"I threw you, Sensei," she said, jumping up and down with excitement.

I sat up and extended my fist. Cindy immediately pounded her fist into mine.

"Very nice throw, Miss Moore," I said, beginning to stand up, "Do you know the name of that throw?"

"Ippon Seoi Nage," she said quickly, before adding, "and it means one arm shoulder throw."

"That's correct," I answered.

She had not actually thrown me of course. She had fit in for the technique correctly, so I rewarded her by jumping into the air and throwing myself. To someone watching who didn't know better, it looked like the little girl tossed me across the room.

I looked around the dojo and saw the rest of the class. Three kids were watching Cindy and me while two of my other students were trying to throw each other in randori, or free practice. They were being watched carefully by Sensei Ito.

Ito was the seventh-degree black belt who instructed me as a child. Now eighty-three years old, he was retired, but had agreed to come back on a part-time basis to help me start and run my own judo club.

It hadn't been my idea to teach. I had never even thought about it. My girlfriend, Becky Foster, had suggested it to me a few months ago. She wanted to learn to defend herself after being in an abusive marriage. Her very large ex-husband and I had had a conversation that ended when he tried to brain me with a heavy wrench. When it was over, I'd left him lying in a pile of hubcaps. Amazed that I could handle someone so much bigger than me caused her to want to be able to do the same.

I'd initially refused. But, after thinking about it for a few weeks, I decided it was worth a try. I told Becky I would do it, but only if there was a kids' class as well. Judo was something that had really helped when I was a boy, and I hoped I might be able to help at least one child in the same way.

My first step was to persuade Sensei Ito to help me. I might have been a second-degree black belt, but Mr. Ito had forgotten more judo than I would ever know. I thought convincing him would be difficult. His own dojo had closed nearly five years ago. I assumed he was enjoying his retirement and was surprised at how quickly he'd agreed to come back. He'd had two conditions though. The first was that he would not have anything to do with the necessary paperwork or finances. I didn't consider this a big deal until I started doing it. Now, I understood his reasoning. It was a lot of work.

The second condition was one I could not accept. He wanted me to call him by his first name, Okada. Since my early childhood, I'd always called him "Sensei" or "Shihan", Japanese words that meant "Honorable Teacher" and "Master Instructor". In my mind, to call him anything else would be disrespectful and just plain wrong.

After several minutes of discussion, we'd reached a compromise. I would call him Okada, but not in class. In the dojo, I would only refer to him as Sensei or Shihan. It felt odd calling him by his first name, but it was well worth it to have his assistance and expertise.

True to his word, Sensei Ito was there every Monday and Wednesday at 3:30pm for the after-school kids' class. We split the adult classes. I took the Tuesday night class and he taught on Thursday night. I often stopped in on Thursday nights, but needed the freedom to address issues that arose with my law office. Ever since the case with the so-called Rockfield Strangler a few months ago, business had been booming.

I was thinking about all of this when I felt a pull on my gi. Little Cindy was trying to throw me again. I had already rewarded her prior good attack by taking a huge fall. In fact, I had taken several of them for her in the last three minutes. I decided that was enough for one night.

I yelled, "Mate," announcing the end of the round.

Cindy stepped back and waited for me. We bowed to each other and she went back against the far wall. She had learned her judo manners well.

All of my students had done well. They understood the importance of etiquette and respect. Judo is a combat sport, but it is also a martial art complete with discipline and life lessons.

I ordered the class to line up. This always caused a few groans because it signaled the end of class. The kids fixed their belts and kneeled along the student line. Sensei Ito and I kneeled at the front of the dojo, facing the students. As the higher rank, Sensei Ito sat to my left.

"A good workout tonight," I announced, "On Wednesday afternoon, we are going to learn a brand-new throw called Sasae Tsuri Komi Ashi. It's a great throw to use when someone charges right at you."

I could see by the looks on their faces that I had their interest. They all wanted to know what this technique was with the fancy long name. I decided not to tell them yet. Best to keep them guessing until the next class.

We went through the process of bowing to one another to end the class. The students offered a thank you using the formal Japanese I had taught them. I gave the proper reply and the students waited for Sensei Ito and me to rise. It was only then that they could stand and go to their waiting parents. We only made them wait for a second or two, and then class was over.

Within fifteen minutes, all of the kids had changed and left with their parents. Sensei Ito departed right after the students. I stuck around to go through the roster on my desk to make sure my attendance notes were correct. After nearly ten minutes of paperwork, I heard a sexy voice from behind me.

"I'm looking for the judo master."

I turned and saw the smile that always made my heart flutter. Becky Foster stood at the entrance to the dojo wearing a tight T-shirt and a pair of black leggings that outlined her in stunning detail.

"Mr. Ito left a few minutes ago," I answered.

"Very funny, wise guy," she said, walking toward me.

I considered making another witty remark but decided better of it. Instead, I just waited until she reached me and then kissed her. It was the right decision. Whenever I kissed her for the first time on a given day, it sent a tingling sensation throughout my body.

Just three months ago, I'd been completely alone. After the death of my wife and our unborn child, I never thought I could be happy again.

I'd thrown myself into a job in New York City that I hated and made a great deal of money—probably more than I would ever be able to spend. Yet, I'd been empty and lonely.

In the space of a week, Becky had come back into my life. We'd grown up together and had been close since childhood.

In high school, I wanted very much to be more than friends, but had been unwilling to take that risk. I always felt with absolute certainty that Becky would have zero interest in me. She always went for the football players and athletes standing at least six feet four inches and weighing two hundred and fifty pounds or more.

When it came time for college, we'd gone our separate ways. Years later, she'd walked into my law office asking for help dealing with her ex-husband, Matt Jordan. She had wanted legal help, though I took the opportunity to physically confront the big jerk. Our first encounter ended with him on the floor.

The second time Matt and I had met, it had very nearly ended in my death and disfigurement. Matt and a friend of his had attacked me as I was getting out of my car. There had been a very tense moment when Matt had a knife held to my face threatening to carve me like a Sunday roast. Even though I survived the attack and left both men unconscious, I suffered a bad concussion and was hospitalized.

When I returned home, Becky insisted on caring for me. I assumed it was out of guilt.

She questioned why I chose to physically confront her ex, and we ended up in an argument. Somehow (I still don't know exactly how), she got me in a fit of anger to admit the feelings I had for her back in our high school days. I remember Becky laughing and calling me a jackass, before explaining that she had gone for Matt only because the man she really wanted had showed no interest. I nearly fell to the floor when she admitted that I was that man. Moments later, we kissed for the first time.

Three months ago, if someone had said I would be this happy, I would have thought that person a fool. Now, I could barely imagine being without her again.

"You still there, Connor?" Becky asked.

"Sure," I replied, forcing myself out of my memories and back to reality. "I wasn't expecting you today."

"Disappointed?" she asked with a mischievous grin.

"Never," I said quickly, "but I thought you were working today."

"No," she replied, "Robert closed The Medallion today. Didn't say why."

The Medallion was Rockfield's most expensive restaurant and Becky worked as the hostess. Opened by Robert Lambert, a gourmet chef, it had been running for about twelve years. The food was good, but Rockfield was like many small cities in upstate New York – poor. It was amazing that the place had been able to survive as long as it had. Yet, it was clear to me that it was only a matter of time before the restaurant failed and Becky was out of a job. I was careful never to discuss this with Becky, though I suspected she knew.

"How about," Becky continued, "we go over to your place, and I cook you one of my famous lasagnas?"

I wasn't about to turn that down. Becky may not have been trained as a gourmet chef like Robert Lambert, but she could make old-fashioned stick-to-your-ribs meals that were just plain awesome.

"Let me just change out of this gi, and we can head right over," I answered.

Her mischievous smile returned.

"Let me help you," she purred, as she put both of her hands into the front of my gi jacket and caressed my chest.

I slid my hand into her silky blond hair, gently pulled her close and kissed her. We were still kissing several moments later when we were both startled by the ringing of my cell phone. Becky was not at all happy when I started to pull away.

"Let it go to voicemail," she whispered.

"I can't," I replied softly. "That particular ring tone means it's a text from the office. Casey only sends me a text message when it's very important."

Casey Franklin is my secretary, though she prefers to be called the office manager. She is so good at her job that I let her choose whatever job title she wishes. Most people think Casey is an opinionated wiseass – and she is – but underneath her sometimes harsh personality and her tendency to swear like a sailor, she is actually a very caring and loving person who would give someone in need her last dollar. I sometimes think her abrasiveness is a way of protecting herself and hiding her natural insecurity, though she would verbally take my head off if I ever suggested such a thing. Regardless, I could not run my law office without her, something Casey reminds me of constantly.

Becky sighed before reaching down and grabbing the phone off my desk. She looked at the screen and immediately seemed puzzled, but said nothing.

"What does it say?" I finally asked

"It says CB," Becky answered. "What the heck does that mean?

"It's a code Casey and I use. It stands for code blue," I said. "It means she needs me to call the office right away.

Taking the phone from Becky, I quickly dialed Casey's direct extension.

"About time," Casey quipped when she answered my call, "Good thing I wasn't bleeding out or something."

"What's the emergency?" I asked, not disguising my annoyance.

"Old Iron Girdle was just here," Casey announced. Old Iron Girdle was her nickname for Ethel Bollenbacher, the stern and rather severe secretary of County Court Judge John Hardy.

"What did Miss Bollenbacher want?" I pressed.

"She retained us to handle a criminal case," Casey answered, "and the arraignment is in less than thirty minutes."

"Wait a minute," I interrupted, "Ethel has been charged with a crime?"

"No," Casey offered, "She wants you to represent Judge John J. Hardy."

"Hardy?" I asked incredulously. "He's the most politically powerful man in the entire county. Cops don't even give him a parking ticket."

"That may be," Casey continued, "But he is facing some serious charges and he's being arraigned tonight down in city court."

My mind was racing. The idea of John Hardy being arrested in Linton County was absurd. He had been district attorney for decades and now served as County Court Judge.

Back in law school, I'd thought my entire career would be spent as a prosecutor sending violent criminals to prison for the rest of their miserable lives.

Right out of law school, I'd taken a job in the Linton County District Attorney's Office working for John Hardy himself. The job paid practically nothing, but I was on top of the world because I was a prosecutor. I'd done as many trials as I could, rose quickly through the ranks, and, after only five years, Hardy appointed me Chief Assistant.

Many considered me Hardy's heir apparent, before I'd lost my wife, Melissa, and my life had come crashing down around me.

I knew Judge Hardy better than most. To say he was an icon in these parts was a huge understatement. Unable to wrap my head around the idea, I finally asked, "What is he charged with?"

Absolutely nothing could have prepared me for what Casey said next.

"They say he killed that filthy child molester, Gilbert Russell."

CHAPTER THREE

"Casey, is this some kind of joke?" I asked, still not quite believing what I had just heard.

"No joke," Casey replied, "Mad Dog Marcus is doing the arraignment in twenty minutes and you know that douchebag isn't going to wait for you."

Mad Dog was another one of Casey's nicknames. This one was for Marcus Marino, the Rockfield City Court Judge. At one time, he had been a respected attorney in the area. Once he got elected to be a judge, however, he transformed from a nice guy into a condescending asshole with delusions of grandeur.

Casey was right that Marino was not going to delay for one second. A few months back, he refused to move a trial even though I had just woken up in the hospital after two days of being semi-conscious. If a near death experience was not a sufficient excuse, I seriously doubted teaching a children's judo class would suffice. "Casey, I'm still at the dojo," I said, "I can't possibly—"

"Go straight to the courthouse, right now," Casey interrupted, "I'll bring your emergency suit and meet you there."

I always kept a clean set of clothes for court in the apartment above my office. I almost never stayed there, but used the apartment to store files, extra clothes, and the office safe.

Ironically, the last time I needed to use one of my emergency suits was before Judge Marino. It was not a memory I cherished, even though I won that trial without even asking a single question.

"Okay, Casey," I replied, "I'm on the way."

I ended the call and tried to explain to Becky why I had to leave. Though her eyes clearly conveyed opposition, she did not fight me on it, much.

"I understand," she said, "but, I'm coming with you."

"There's no need," I answered immediately. "You'll just..."

I stopped talking mid-sentence as she held her palm up to my face in a classic talk-to-the-hand gesture.

"I'm coming with you," she announced. When I did not reply, she continued. "You know I love criminal cases."

That was certainly true. Over the last few months, we had sat together many a night watching *Forensic Files* and *NCIS*. Becky was always stopping by our local bookstore and buying true crime novels. I knew there was no point in arguing. She was coming.

"All right," I relented, "Let's go."

We hurried out to my Cherokee and headed for court. We got there in just under ten minutes. I was more than a little embarrassed to approach the metal detectors just outside of the courtroom wearing just my judo gi and sneakers. The officer checking us in kept from laughing, but it was obviously a considerable effort. He clearly wanted to make a comment. Fortunately, he either couldn't think of one or couldn't do it with a straight face.

Just beyond, I could see Casey holding my suit and shoes.

Her smirk showed just how much she was enjoying my embarrassment.

"You could have met me outside," I said disdainfully.

"And miss the look on your face?" Casey replied with a big smile. "No way."

I took the garment bag and shoes without further comment and turned toward the men's room. It was the only place to change. Just before I entered, I looked through the window of the courtroom door. All I could see were the seats for the audience. They were almost entirely filled with reporters. Obviously, someone had alerted them. I had a pretty good idea who it was.

Five minutes later, I walked back out of the bathroom wearing a light gray suit and royal blue tie. My gi, belt, and sneakers were stuffed into the garment bag. I handed it to Casey.

"You should have worn the Chuck Norris outfit." Casey offered sarcastically, "Mad Dog would have loved it."

Becky giggled at the remark, but stopped when I shot her a quick look. It was obvious that both of them wanted to laugh openly. Resigned to defeat once again, I turned and walked into the courtroom.

As soon as I was through the door, I looked toward the front of the room and saw Judge Hardy standing before the bench. His hands were cuffed behind him. He was wearing a suit, so I knew they had not taken him to the county jail yet. Marino must have called the case early.

Standing on Hardy's left and right were two large sheriff's deputies. At the prosecutor's table was none other than District Attorney Worthington himself. He was dressed in a suit that must have cost several thousand dollars. It was highly unusual for the district attorney to handle a simple arraignment in local court. That was a job for first-year assistants. The fact that

Worthington was here confirmed my earlier suspicion that he was the one who had informed the press of the arrest and court appearance.

I was also certain that Worthington had arranged for the two deputies to stand next to Hardy. It was part of an obvious ploy to convey that the defendant was a dangerous killer who had to be contained. It was almost farcical.

I decided it was my job to not only represent John Hardy, but also to ruin Worthington's photo op.

"My client pleads not guilty, Your Honor," I shouted out, as I walked briskly toward the bench.

All heads in the courtroom turned toward me, including that of the judge and district attorney. Neither of them appeared happy to see me, though Hardy did. He smiled broadly when I stood next to him.

"This proceeding has already started, Mr. Phelan," Marino bellowed.

"My apologies, Your Honor," I offered, before he could say another syllable. "I was just retained in the last twenty minutes or so and I came straight here."

"How could you have been retained?" Worthington shouted, "The prisoner was arrested and taken straight to this court."

"That is privileged information, Mr. Worthington," I said, without even looking at him, "but I can assure the court that I have been retained to represent County Court Judge John J. Hardy."

Judge Marino picked up a manila folder from his desk and made a demonstration of looking through it.

"I do not see a Notice of Appearance in my file from your office, Mr. Phelan," the judge announced in a demeaning tone. "Court rules are quite specific on this."

This was a really cheap move by the judge. While a notice

of appearance was required, it was understood as part of custom and practice that lawyers were often retained at the last minute for arraignments. The formal notice would almost always be filed later. Marino was making this statement in an attempt to degrade me in front of the press.

"I do not have one either, Your Honor," Worthington announced in his nasal drone. "As such, I formally object to—"

He did not get to finish his statement, as he was interrupted when the door from the judge's chambers opened and the judge's secretary walked through carrying some papers. She went straight to the judge and handed them to him. She whispered something to Judge Marino and then turned and walked back out through the same door.

"It would appear," Judge Marino announced, his voice almost expressing disappointment, "that your office has indeed filed a Notice of Appearance as required."

I looked out at the front row of spectators where Becky and Casey were sitting. Casey had a very satisfied smile on her face. When she saw me looking, she just winked. I really couldn't run my office without her; a fact I was sure she would mention soon.

I looked back to the bench just as Judge Marino started speaking again.

"Mr. Phelan, why didn't you tell me you had already filed the document with my clerk?"

"Well, Your Honor," I replied, "I knew better than to interrupt you, and Mr. Worthington chose to make his objection—"

"Okay, fair enough," the judge interjected. "The court recognizes you as defense counsel."

"Just a moment," Worthington spoke up. "My office has not been served with that document, judge. I therefore must renew my strenuous objection..."

"J. Robert Worthington?" a woman's voice asked. "This is for you."

Worthington and I turned to see who had spoken. To our astonishment, Casey was standing right behind the prosecutor. In her outstretched hand was a white envelope. When the district attorney took the envelope from her, Casey spoke again.

"You have been served, sir."

Without another word, she walked back to the front row and sat down.

I could not believe Casey's audacity. To interrupt a court proceeding was always unwise, but to do so in Judge Marino's court risked a finding of contempt and a trip to the county jail. Yet, the look on Worthington's face was beyond satisfying. I wasn't sure when I got back to the office if I was going to yell at Casey or give her a raise.

For several long moments, nobody said anything. The silence was eventually broken by Judge Marino.

"Young lady?" he asked, addressing Casey directly.

"Yes, sir?" Casey asked calmly, as she got to her feet.

"May I presume that the envelope you just gave the district attorney contains Mr. Phelan's Notice of Appearance for this case?"

"Yes, your Honor."

Marino looked to me for confirmation. I just nodded.

"She is your secretary?" he asked.

"Yes, Your—" I started to say.

"Office Manager," Casey corrected sternly, causing many in the court to laugh.

Expecting the judge to explode, I decided to speak first.

"Your Honor, I apologize for my—"

"No need, counselor," Marino said, cutting me off. "My legal secretary insists on being called 'Executive Assistant'."

Everyone in the court except District Attorney Worthington

laughed until Judge Marino lightly tapped his gavel on the bench.

"Okay, let's get back to business, shall we?" he said, as he turned toward Worthington. "Your motion is denied."

The look of barely contained rage and frustration on Worthington's face was priceless.

"Defense counsel has announced a plea of not guilty, but we actually have not even read the charges yet," Marino said.

"That's fine, Your Honor, but the defense waives formal reading of the charges and enters a plea of not guilty," I said.

"Just a moment," Worthington barked, "I want the formal charges read aloud."

This was clearly a ploy for the assembled media. This was why he had made sure to appear personally for the arraignment. I was not about to oblige his ego.

"Your Honor," I offered, "it is the defendant's right to have the charges read or to waive the reading. We waive."

Worthington opened his mouth to object, but Marino spoke first.

"I agree," he said, beginning to write in his file, "a plea of not guilty is entered and the defendant..."

"Excuse me, judge," Worthington whined.

Marino's head snapped up. His eyes revealed great displeasure at being interrupted.

"What is it, Mr. Worthington?" Marino responded in a voice scarcely above a whisper that barely contained his growing annoyance.

"The People object to the setting of bail in this case," Worthington said in a loud voice, obviously making sure all of the reporters could hear him. "The defendant is charged with First Degree Murder and—"

"Pardon me, judge," I interrupted.

"I am speaking!" Worthington roared. "Just who do you think you are?"

"I think," I continued in a pronounced staccato voice, "that I am someone who has grown tired of your grandstanding."

"How dare you?" he demanded. "I am the duly elected district attorney of this—"

"And this is *my* courtroom," Judge Marino finally exploded. "Both of you will address your remarks to me and me alone. Is that understood?"

"Yes, judge," I replied.

Worthington nodded, but said nothing.

"Now," the judge continued, "what were you saying Mr. Phelan?"

Worthington inhaled sharply, but before he could speak, Marino threw him a look that made it crystal clear that he would not tolerate one word of protest. Worthington again nodded in acquiescence. The judge then turned back to me.

"As much as I wish my client ordered released, judge," I said, "New York State Law does not permit a local court to set bail on a murder charge."

I took a second to look over at Worthington as I cleared my throat. His face was flushed with anger and embarrassment. He had either forgotten or did not know the law on setting bail.

"That being said, judge, I will be filing a bail application to the appropriate court within the hour."

"And I will be there to oppose it," Worthington announced loudly.

Marino shook his head in exasperation before picking up his gavel and banging the bench.

"The defendant is remanded. I am scheduling the preliminary hearing six days from today. We are adjourned," he pronounced, before quickly standing and heading for his door.

From behind me, I heard the court bailiff call for all

assembled to stand. People were still rising when Marino slammed the door closed behind him.

As the two deputies started to escort Hardy from the court, I leaned in and whispered in his ear.

"Don't speak to anyone, John. I'll be back shortly to talk to you before they take you to the jail."

"Connor, my boy," he said in a loud voice for the press to hear. "I'm an innocent man."

Then, he leaned in to me and whispered, "I know I'm in good hands."

I watched as they walked him out of the court with reporters screaming questions at him. To my relief, John gave no comment.

Becky came bounding up to me and hugged me.

"Brilliant as always," she said.

Casey followed carrying my garment bag. I waited for the comment I knew was coming.

"Executive Assistant." she said. "I like the sound of that."

CHAPTER FOUR

I asked Becky and Casey to wait for me as I headed for the holding cells. I wanted to speak with John Hardy before he left for the jail. Unfortunately, one of the deputies blocked my entrance.

"Sorry, counselor," he announced, "but the prisoner is being prepared for transport."

"Before you leave, may I speak with John Hardy for a minute or two?"

"No, sir," he answered stoically.

I was fairly sure that this was Worthington's doing. It was the type of disrespectful pettiness for which he was well known. However, it was not the deputy's fault and I saw no reason to pressure him. I wished him a nice day and walked away.

Becky and Casey saw me heading for the exit and followed. When I got to my Cherokee, I turned and waited until they caught up.

"Becky, please go with Casey. She'll drop you off at the dojo so you can get your car."

She started to protest, but I cut her off.

"I'll pick you up later tonight and we'll get some dinner.

Okay? Right now, I have to get over to the county jail and talk to Hardy."

Becky smiled, leaned in, and kissed me on the cheek. "You still want that lasagna?" she asked.

"You bet," I answered, "but I don't know how long I'm going to be. Maybe instead we can—"

"Stop by The Cardinal for a quick bite," she said, finishing my sentence.

It was really unnerving sometimes how easily she could read my mind. She seemed to be able to know my words before they even formed in my head. Was I really that predictable?

The Cardinal is a tavern owned by my best friend, Eddie Astorino. It was where I often went for a drink or a meal, especially when I had a particularly tough case. The fact that it was usually open late was also very helpful.

"You don't mind?" I asked, giving Becky one of my best smiles.

"No," she said through an exasperated sigh, "I understand. You have to do some big-shot lawyer stuff first."

"Something like that," I confirmed.

"Don't be too late," she said with an impish grin.

I turned to Casey.

"After you drop Becky off, get back to the office and—"

"Call Mr. Wonderful," she said sarcastically.

There seemed to be no limit to the number of nicknames Casey had for people. This one was for Dom Bryce, my investigator. Dom is one of the best investigators I have ever worked with, and a great friend. He worked for many years in the County Sheriff's Office, retiring as a detective lieutenant. After that, he worked as an investigator for John Hardy when he was district attorney. When Hardy moved up to County Court Judge and Worthington was elected D.A., Dom resigned immediately, choosing never to work for a man he described tenderly as a "no good lying fuck".

Ever since I opened my law office, I had spent many an evening with Dom at my home reviewing evidence, drinking beer, and eating pizza. I always had to be careful not to let Dom order the pizza. He liked those horrible anchovies.

"Right," I continued, "Tell Dom I need him to get me everything he can on the murder of Gilbert Russell and what evidence Worthington has on John Hardy."

"Yes, sir", she replied with a mock salute, starting to head for her car.

"One more thing," I announced, "Tomorrow, you and I are going to have a conversation about proper courtroom etiquette."

Casey put on her best angelic face and replied, "Me? I thought I was perfectly charming."

Becky laughed and I made a sound something like "harumpf", as the ladies walked to Casey's car. Casey opened the driver's door and then looked back at me, her usual smirk returning to her face.

"Besides," she said, "you can't tell me that prick Worthington didn't have it coming."

"No doubt," I answered, before they drove away.

Twenty minutes later, I arrived at the Linton County Jail. It was an old stone and brick building that had been in use for over a century. It was badly in need of repair or demolition. State officials every so often made noise about wanting the county to build a new facility, but Linton County always avoided the issue and the huge price tag that went with it.

I parked in the visitors' lot and made my way into the building and to the front desk. Sitting at the desk behind a Plexiglas window was a deputy sheriff who was clearly overweight and ready for retirement. He was reading a newspaper and leaning back on a wooden chair that was giving its all. He did not even look up as he spoke.

"Can I help you?" he asked.

"Yes," I said, "I'm Connor Phelan. I would like to speak with my client, County Court Judge John Hardy."

That got his attention. He dropped his newspaper as he sat up and the chair clunked back into place.

"Just a moment, sir," he said as he dialed his phone. A moment later, he spoke again, "Sheriff Sanders?" he said nervously, "Mr. Phelan is here to see the judge." He listened for a moment, said, "Yes, sir," and hung up the phone. Then he looked back at me.

"The Sheriff will be right with you, sir."

I thanked the deputy and walked over to the far wall where a row of chairs were lined up. I sat down and waited. I was just thinking how odd it was that the Sheriff himself would be involved with an attorney-inmate visit when the large metal door all the way in the back of the building opened and Sheriff Harvey Sanders came walking out.

Harvey Sanders had been the sheriff for decades. He came from an old family in the county that had always been in law enforcement, though he hardly looked the part. He was about five feet six inches tall with thin gray hair combed straight back. He wore small, round glasses. He was neither heavy nor muscular. His frame and appearance seemed more like an accountant than a lawman.

"Hello, Connor," he said, sticking out his hand, "Nice to see you."

His voice was authoritative in a grandfatherly way.

"You always come out when an attorney wants to see an inmate?" I asked with a smile.

Sanders gave the smile right back. "Only when that prisoner is John Hardy," he replied.

He asked me to follow him and I did so. We went through the large metal door and immediately turned right. This was unusual, as I knew from prior visits with incarcerated clients that the cells were off to the left and down the stairs. I had never been this way. I said nothing and continued to walk with him.

Eventually, we arrived at the Sheriff's office. The office was fairly large. A nice executive-style wooden desk and high-back chair faced the door. In front of the desk were two leather chairs. Sitting in one of them was John Hardy. He was still dressed in his suit and his hands were no longer cuffed. In one of his hands, Hardy held a glass of what appeared to be Scotch. He stood as soon as he saw me.

"Connor, my boy," he said jovially, "come on in and have a seat."

In court, Hardy's face had been decidedly pale. Now, the usual redness had returned to his cheeks. This created quite a contrast to the thick snowy-white hair on top of his head.

We shook hands and I took a seat in the vacant chair next to the judge.

John grabbed a bottle of fifteen-year-old Glenlivet off the sheriff's desk. "You want a drink?" he asked.

"No," I answered, "I drink Irish whiskey."

"Suit yourself," Hardy replied, pouring more of the amber liquid into his glass.

John J. Hardy had been district attorney and county court judge. He was the most powerful and influential man in the county. It must be nice, I thought, to have such clout that you could be accused of murder and sit in the sheriff's office shooting the breeze and drinking expensive Scotch.

"This is quite a jail cell," I finally said.

"You don't think I'm gonna put John in one of them cells, do you?" Sanders asked. "Those are for criminals."

"Forgive me, Sheriff," I offered, "but my client has been accused of murder."

He made a dismissive gesture and grunted. "Let me tell you something, son," Sanders said in a very direct tone while pointing his finger at me, "I may have to keep John Hardy in this building, but I am not putting him in one of those filthy fucking cells when I know God damn well that the charges against him are a great big pile of horse shit."

Hardy burst out laughing.

"Connor," he said, "Old Harv and I go back more years than I can remember. Don't worry about me. He ain't gonna put me in general population with the people I sentenced. He's not a sniveling little asshole like Worthington."

I started to speak but Hardy held up his hand to stop me.

"Besides, I expect to be out of here in a few hours once you file my bail application in State Supreme Court."

"John, it's already nearly 7:30pm," I protested, "All of the judges have gone home. You're probably stuck here until tomorrow morning."

"Nonsense," he roared. "just give me the phone."

The sheriff reached into his pocket and gave Hardy a cell phone. As Hardy punched in the number, I thought to myself that this whole thing was like something out of *The Andy Griffith Show.*

After about five minutes of barking into the phone, he handed the cell back to Harvey Sanders.

"Judge Francis O'Connor will meet you in one hour in his chambers," Hardy said. "He'll call the district attorney to let him know. Worthington will scream his head off, but Frannie will order me released to house arrest. I'll have to wear one of them ankle monitors, but I'll be home."

"Well," I said, "That was easy enough."

When Hardy did not reply, I continued. "John, you and I need to talk alone. You may be able to avoid a cell and get yourself sent home, but Worthington is not going to just dismiss these charges."

"That much I know," Hardy replied. "Can you give us a few minutes, Harv?"

The Sheriff smiled. "Sure John, you got ten minutes. But I'm taking my Scotch with me."

The two men laughed, and Sanders left, closing the door behind him.

Since I had limited time, I got right to the point.

"John, how could Worthington possibly think you killed Russell?"

"It's my own fucking fault, Connor," he replied, a hint of both anger and sadness creeping into his voice. "I got cocky and made that stupid statement in court that Russell should have been taken out and hanged. Now, that exact thing has happened. It was just damn stupid of me to—"

"Wait a minute," I interrupted, "You and I both know that a remark like that isn't enough to get an arrest warrant. Besides, everyone and his mother were talking all over town about how Russell should have been hanged, shot, beaten, or whatever."

"That's true enough," Hardy conceded.

"They have to have found some other piece of direct evidence against you, John. The question is what."

"Damned if I know," Hardy offered, "but it must be something pretty convincing if Marcus signed the warrant."

I raised my eyebrows at the comment, but Hardy waived me off.

"Oh, Marcus is a horse's ass," he continued, "but he's not dishonest or crooked. He likes tearing people down, but he won't break the law to do it. No, there must be something."

Hardy and I spoke for several minutes. He promised me he would not talk to anyone about the case or reveal anything we discussed, not even to an old friend like Harvey Sanders.

There was a knock at the door signaling that our time was up. As I got up to leave, Hardy grabbed me by the arm.

"Connor, listen to me," the old judge said, his voice cracking slightly, showing the first signs of fear or apprehension. "You know I didn't kill him."

"I know, John," I replied, but Hardy just grabbed my arm harder trying to solidify his point.

"I've seen innocent men end up in prison before," he continued. "In this county, nobody can touch me. Even in county jail, I can sit here and drink Scotch. But, in state prison, I've got nothing and no one to protect me."

He stared at me intently and I could see fear resonating in his pale eyes. It was the only time I could ever remember seeing John Hardy appear vulnerable.

Hardy cleared his throat before continuing.

"You were my best assistant district attorney, Connor. I knew you as a boy and have seen you grow into a man. You've become the best attorney I've ever known. There is nobody I trust more to help me."

He paused for a moment to stifle the emotion growing within him that he did not want released. After a few seconds, Hardy let go of my arm.

"Let me know what you find out," he said softly.

I nodded my head and then walked to the door. I opened it and started through. I took one look back and saw the powerful county court judge drain the rest of the Scotch in his glass. What I noticed most was how much his hand trembled as he did so.

CHAPTER FIVE

I left the county jail and headed straight to my office. As I drove, I kept seeing that look in Hardy's eyes and the trembling of his hand as he drank. It replayed in my mind over and over again.

John Hardy was a mentor. He taught me the practice of law. His style was always one of supreme confidence and strength. No matter what the legal dilemma or how difficult the case, nothing ever seemed to bother him. He was a rock.

What I saw when I looked in his eyes was a mixture of fear and almost helplessness. It was something I knew I would not soon forget. He was terrified of going to prison, a place where he would be nothing but a tired old man with a target on his back; a place where people he sentenced to life terms would seek hideous revenge designed to cause him both pain and humiliation.

I vowed to myself that I was not going to let that happen. I had no idea what evidence Worthington had or how strong his case was, but I was going to make sure he did not get a conviction. To do that, I had to not only prove John Hardy's innocence, but also figure out who really killed Gilbert Russell.

Since pretty much everyone in the county hated the man and wanted him dead, I certainly had plenty of suspects.

When I got back to the office, Casey was at her desk. I was slightly surprised as the office closes at five. Casey was free to go home at that time, but she had decided to stick around. I made a quick mental note to make sure she got a little extra in her paycheck next week. I also expected at some point in the very near future that she would make the very same suggestion.

"I called Mr. Wonderful," she offered as soon as she saw me. "He said he would get right on it and would be by tomorrow morning with whatever he found."

"Thanks," I replied dismissively and walked past her into my office. I was not in the mood to talk and just wanted to sit in my chair and prepare the papers I would need for Judge O'Connor.

On my desk waiting for me was a hot mug of coffee with cream and sugar, just the way I liked it. Next to the coffee was a manila folder. I sat down and opened it. Inside was a bail application form. Casey heard me tell Judge Marino that I was going to file a bail application, so she had returned to the office and filled it out. The only thing it needed was my signature.

As usual, Casey had everything ready to go. I smiled to myself and called her into the office. Casey could drive me crazy, but as good a secretary, office manager, or executive assistant as she was, I still had to remember that she was only twenty-five years old. Sometimes her emotions still got the better of her.

Hell, I thought, I'm forty-one and I still do that on occasion.

She came right in and sat in one of the chairs in front of my desk. She had a look on her face like a kid called into the principal's office.

"Connor, I'm sorry about court today," she said apologetically, "I know I shouldn't have spoken out to the judge and given Worthington those papers, but that guy is such a douchebag and I—"

"Casey," I said loudly, holding up my hands to stop her, "You did fine today. Thank you for having hot coffee and my papers ready for me. It gives me some time to just sit and relax."

She looked at me apprehensively, almost expecting the other shoe to drop. We both knew she had overstepped in court, but it was also clear between us that she would not do so again. It was unnecessary for me to actually say it.

"You've put in a long day today," I said, "Go on home. I'll take it from here."

"You don't have to ask me twice," she replied, standing and heading for the door. She paused in the doorway and looked back at me. "You sure?" she asked.

"Yes," I said, "I'll see you tomorrow."

When she paused for another second, I added, "Yes, Casey, you will be paid for the overtime."

Casey smiled warmly and left.

I leaned back in my chair and slowly drank my coffee. When I finished it, I called Becky.

"It's about time," she answered, "I was beginning to think you had forgotten about me."

"Sorry," I replied, "It's been a busy evening."

I brought her up to date on everything and I explained that I had to be in Judge O'Connor's chambers in twenty-five minutes for the bail application.

"So, pick me up," she said cheerily, "I'll go with you and then we can get some food. I'm starving."

I knew better than to argue with her about how boring a bail application would be. She would just tell me about the latest true crime book she was reading.

"Okay," I finally said, "I'll be there in ten minutes."

After hanging up the phone, I gathered my papers and

headed out. I locked up the office and jumped in my Cherokee. I made it to Becky's front door about a minute earlier than I had predicted.

When Becky opened the door, I couldn't speak for a few seconds. She had changed her clothes. The sexy leggings and T-shirt had been replaced with blue slacks and a white Aran sweater. Her hair was in a pony-tail that hung over her right shoulder. She looked absolutely stunning.

"Hello?' she asked, bringing me out of my momentary stupor.

"Oh, sorry," I said quickly, "just lost in thought."

She said nothing, though the look in her eyes told me she knew I had not been lost in thought at all. In fact, for those few seconds, my mind had completely shut down. It was unnerving, but more than worth it.

I escorted her to the car and we headed off to see the judge.

When we got to the courthouse and parked, I saw a Rockfield Police officer waiting at the main door. The court was normally closed at this time of night. But, even from jail, John Hardy had been able to get the building opened and have a judge and officer available.

At the door, I could see that the officer's name plate identified him as Patrolman Chandler. He greeted Becky and I cordially.

"Good evening, Mr. Phelan," he said.

"Ma'am", he continued, as he glanced at Becky and tipped his hat slightly.

"I'm here to see Judge O'Connor," I offered.

"Yes, sir," Chandler replied politely. "The judge and Mr. Worthington are upstairs. Please follow me.

He led us up the main stairs to the third floor. When we arrived at Judge O'Connor's chambers, Chandler knocked lightly on the door as he opened it.

"Your Honor?" he asked, "Mr. Phelan is here."

"Show him in," came the reply from within.

The officer opened the door for us and beckoned us in. Beyond, Judge O'Connor was seated at his desk. He was not wearing his judge's robe or a suit jacket. He had clearly come directly from home and was wearing casual clothes. O'Connor was completely bald, though it was not entirely clear if this was by nature or razor.

District Attorney Worthington was seated in one of the three chairs in front of the judge's desk. He did not seem pleased to see me.

"Please sit down, Mr. Phelan," the judge directed.

O'Connor smiled when he spotted Becky. "Good evening," he said warmly. "Please have a seat as well."

As we sat, the judge said, "Mr. Phelan, you are of course acquainted with District Attorney Worthington?"

"Yes, judge," I replied, extending my hand to the district attorney.

Worthington was attired in his usual multi-thousand-dollar suit with a Rolex watch and matching gold cufflinks. He did not shake my hand. Instead, he sneered, "We have met."

The petty rudeness didn't really bother me. I had offered my hand just out of manners and habit. If O'Connor noted the snub, he didn't mention it. Instead, he moved right to business.

"All right, gentlemen," he said. "We are here to discuss whether to grant bail to John Hardy."

"Your Honor," Worthington snarled. "The People strenuously oppose any bail in this matter. The defendant in this case is charged with intentional murder. And I feel—"

"The court is aware of the charges against John Hardy," O'Connor interrupted, clearly annoyed at Worthington's tone. "The issue here is whether the accused will appear in court."

"Your Honor," Worthington interjected, showing no

intentions of backing down. "This defendant is a cold-blooded murderer. He stated in court that he wanted Gilbert Russell to be taken from the courtroom and hanged in the town square. Within days, he did exactly that. Such a violent criminal deserves no bail and no mercy."

When Worthington finished his tirade, the judge just looked at me for comment.

"Pardon me, judge," I said, "but there has been no trial and no conviction. Last I knew, people accused of crimes in this country are innocent until proven guilty. As for bail—"

"John Hardy is as guilty as hell!" Worthington shouted.

Before the judge could scold the district attorney for shouting and swearing, I tried to turn up the heat.

"You don't have one scrap of evidence against him," I said mockingly. "You're making this whole thing up."

"Then explain to me how John Hardy's hair was found on the victim," Worthington screamed back, before suddenly realizing he had said too much. Though he would eventually have to turn over his evidence in discovery, he had no obligation to disclose it now. It was a foolish mistake on his part. His face turned even more red with his embarrassment.

Now, thanks to Worthington's loss of temper, I knew the basis for Hardy's arrest. If some of his hair *had* been found on Gilbert Russell's body, it would be very incriminating evidence. If they were able to get DNA from that hair and it matched Hardy, it would be absolutely damning evidence.

Though I was pleased to have tricked the district attorney into revealing his case, I was very concerned that Worthington might just have the cards to win. I knew without question that Hardy was innocent. I just wasn't sure I could prove it.

"When we get to trial, I will do just that," I boasted, trying to maintain my confidence.

"Direct your comments to me please," O'Connor ordered.

"Yes, judge," I replied. "Sir, Judge John Hardy is a respected and well-known member of this community. His family has been here for over a hundred years. He is looking forward to clearing his name and resuming his duties as county court judge. He will turn in his passport and take whatever steps the court may require should you grant—"

"Judge," Worthington interrupted yet again, "Hardy had the means, the opportunity, and the motive."

"Motive? You want to talk about motive?" I asked incredulously. "Gilbert Russell was despised by nearly everyone in the county."

"But, not everyone in the county threatened to hang him like Hardy did!" the district attorney yelled.

"Are you kidding me?" I asked. "Every person in every bar and restaurant was talking about shooting him, stabbing him, or beating him to death."

"But Hardy is the one who did it," Worthington insisted, jumping to his feet.

"If you really want to see someone with motive, Mr. Worthington," I challenged, "take a look in the mirror."

"What?"

"You wanted to run for State Attorney General. It was your incompetence that got Russell released from prison," I continued. "That ended any chance you had of ever holding state office. You had the oldest motive in the book. Revenge."

"How dare you?" Worthington thundered. "Don't you know who I am? I'm—"

"A jealous, arrogant fool," I said, finishing his sentence.

"That's enough, gentlemen," O'Connor announced, banging his fist on the table. "Let's cut the grandstanding. It's late and I want to go home. I certainly don't want to hear this crap."

When the district attorney opened his mouth to speak,

O'Connor pointed his finger at him and said, "One word and you'll need to file your own bail application. Now, sit down."

Worthington glared at the judge, but eventually resumed his seat.

The judge then started writing in his file and spoke as he wrote.

"John J. Hardy is hereby ordered to home confinement. He will wear an ankle monitor at all times and will not leave his home except to attend court or upon further judicial order. He will turn in his passport to the court as well."

He finished writing and slammed his pen on his desk. He stood up and took his coat that had been on the chair behind him.

"Show yourselves out," he ordered, "I'm going home." Without another word, he walked out of the room and slammed the door behind him.

As I stood to leave, Worthington spoke again.

"I guarantee you, Phelan, that the *Honorable* John J. Hardy is going to spend the rest of his miserable life in state prison."

I decided to ignore his arrogant boasts and started moving toward the door. However, Worthington was not about to let it go.

"I'm going to try this case myself, Phelan," he shouted. "I'm going to teach you a thing or two about the law."

I stopped and took a breath. Then, I turned and walked over to him. I got right in his face so I could look him squarely in the eyes.

"The day you can teach me anything about the practice of law is the day I have to retire," I said coldly. "You couldn't carry my briefcase."

Worthington sneered, but backed away. Without another word, he left.

When I turned to get my briefcase, Becky was standing next to me snickering.

"Something funny?" I asked.

"No," she said flashing her dazzling smile, "but you certainly know how to make friends and influence people."

CHAPTER SIX

B ecky and I wasted little time leaving the courthouse. Officer Chandler was nowhere to be found, and the door locked behind us as we left. Neither of us spoke until we were back in my Jeep.

"So, what's next?" Becky asked enthusiastically.

"We eat," I answered immediately. When Becky just stared at me blankly, I added, "I'm starving."

"Me too," she said, "but I meant what's next with the case?"

"Nothing for tonight. Tomorrow, Dom will get whatever information he can about the prosecution's case."

I started the car and pulled out of the lot. Becky was not about to let it go.

"I can't believe they have hair evidence," she offered. When I did not reply, she continued, "Do you think they have DNA too?"

"I don't know," I answered after a few seconds of silence.

I drove several blocks before Becky spoke again.

"You're worried, aren't you?" she asked.

I stopped at a red light and turned to face her.

"If they really have hair or DNA evidence, getting Hardy cleared is going to be very difficult," I said. "Forensics don't lie."

"Is it possible he actually killed him?" Becky asked.

"No," I said quickly. "That's not possible."

I turned back to the wheel, saw the light had turned green, and started the car forward again. Yet, there was just the slightest doubt nagging at me. Hardy had said Russell deserved to die.

"If it were up to me, you would be taken from this courtroom and hanged in the town square," he had said.

That exact thing he said had come to pass. Furthermore, the prosecution apparently had found some of Hardy's hair on the victim. That put him at the scene of the hanging. If he had not killed him, how the hell did his hair get on the victim's body, I wondered.

Was it possible? Could Hardy have taken his role as judge and deliverer of justice too far? Had he made himself judge and executioner? He was a powerful man used to getting whatever he wanted. Had he taken it to the next level of entitlement and privilege?

No, I decided. It was not possible. John Hardy was a lot of things, but a murderer was not one of them.

Though I had made my decision on the matter, the doubt still remained like a candle flickering in the far distance; too far away to see clearly, but enough to keep your attention.

It bothered me that I could not erase it from my mind.

"You'll win the case in the end," Becky suddenly declared.

"How do you know that?" I asked.

Becky smiled. "Because you're the big-shot lawyer," she answered.

I couldn't help but laugh a little. Becky had that quality about her. She could make me smile in almost any circumstance, no matter how dire.

To be more accurate, she had a way of drawing out my emotions in various forms: happiness, frustration, anger, or even fear. I'd always prided myself on my poker face. I could hide my true feelings and thoughts from anyone — except her. Her brown eyes and beautiful smile just broke through every defense and left me transparent right to my soul. I was glad she never became a lawyer. I don't think I would have ever won a case against her.

I pulled into the parking lot of The Cardinal. Based on the number of parked cars, it appeared it was a slow night for the tavern.

I got out and walked to the passenger door. When Becky got out, I extended my arm and escorted her into the restaurant.

Inside, Eddie Astorino was standing behind the bar cleaning glasses. He was wearing a red T-shirt and blue jeans with his usual white apron over the top. His head had a shadow of brown whiskers. He had shaved his head ever since he noticed a bald spot several years ago and tonight looked like he had a five o'clock shadow on his scalp.

When he saw us, he brightened right up.

"Hey, Clubber," he shouted.

Ever since we were in high school together, Eddie had called me Clubber. If asked why, he would tell a fanciful story of me knocking out a school athlete with one punch. The truth was I had defended myself and taken the guy down with a basic judo technique. Eddie preferred his version, but almost never mentioned that the fight came about because he had taken the huge football player's girlfriend to the dance as his date.

He could sometimes drive me crazy; yet, there were few people more willing to hit me between the eyes with the truth than Eddie. When Becky and I had first started dating, I was not sure I was ready. I hadn't even considered another woman since Melissa, my wife, had died.

Eddie all but grabbed me and shook me. He reminded me through his swearing and cursing that Melissa had been dead for ten years. He reminded me of how crazy I had been about Becky in high school. Eddie basically made me feel like a complete idiot for even thinking about calling it off with Becky.

I had taken his advice, continued the relationship, and never regretted it even once. I owed him big for that.

"Miss Becky," Eddie continued in a fake and rather poor southern accent. "You are looking ravishing this evening."

"Why thank you," she replied, highlighting each word.

"Here for drinks or dinner?" Eddie asked.

I opened my mouth to speak, but Becky beat me to it.

"Both," she announced.

"Then, follow me," Eddie replied, starting to walk around the bar.

"This will do just fine," Becky said, hopping on to a barstool.

Eddie smiled. "I love this lady," he said. "No idea what she sees in you, Clubber," he continued, giving Becky a big wink.

"I don't know either," I offered, both as a joke and, in a very real way, as truth. I never would say it openly, but I always felt Becky could do better than me.

Once again, almost seeing right through me, Becky looked my way and said "Big-shot attorneys turn me on."

"No accounting for taste," Eddie and I said at the same time.

We all laughed and I sat on the barstool next to Becky.

"My lady," Eddie continued, "what'll it be?"

Becky ordered a beer. When Eddie held up two fingers to ask if I wanted one, I shook my head.

"Give me a Glendalough," I said, "and make it a double."

"A double?" Eddie asked as he pulled down the bottle. "Whenever you order a double, it means trouble."

He poured whiskey into a glass for me and into a second for himself. He handed me the glass, and raised his in mock salute.

"Saluti," he toasted in a terrible Italian accent before drinking.

"Slàinte, mhaith" I answered in my best Irish brogue, and took a strong draw from the glass. As the whiskey hit my stomach, I felt its warmth rise up into my chest and arms.

Becky raised her beer and offered her own toast.

"Ashes to ashes, and dust to dust. If it weren't for our ass, our belly would bust."

Eddie burst out laughing and nearly fell over backwards. It was rare that Becky swore. So, when she did, it usually caught everyone by surprise.

When he recovered, he raised his glass to Becky and said, "Here's hoping Clubber is never stupid enough to let you go."

"I'll drink to that," she answered.

I made sure to raise my glass as well.

After finishing his sip, Eddie looked back at me and then to Becky.

"So, what's the matter with him?" he asked Becky.

"He has a tough case," she replied.

Eddie's face flashed with understanding. "You're representing the judge, aren't you?" he asked.

When I nodded yes, Eddie became angry. "Look, don't get me wrong," he started, "that perverted piece of crap got exactly what he deserved, but I don't believe for a second that the judge did it."

"I don't either, Eddie," I said, taking another mouthful of Glendalough, "but if they have the evidence Worthington claims—"

"That guy is a walking, talking rectum," Eddie interrupted, causing Becky to laugh and spit out some of her beer.

"Maybe," I answered, "but that rectum could win if he has the evidence he claims."

"What has he got?" Eddie asked.

Before I could reply, Becky jumped right in. "Hair evidence," she said.

Eddie laughed and pointed at his head. "As you can see, I don't offer much on hair."

I lifted my glass. "To Eddie's bald head," I toasted, hoping to change the subject.

They both raised their glasses and laughed.

Eddie knew me well enough to know that it was time to move on. So, he asked us for our orders. Becky requested a maple glazed pork chop with a mashed sweet potato. I ordered linguini and red clam sauce. That particular entrée was one of the recipes Eddie had inherited from his late mother. It was by far the best thing on the menu.

As we ate, there was little conversation. My mind was still locked on Worthington's statement that they had hair evidence. I didn't know if it was just a similar hair, which was no big deal, or if there was a DNA match, which would be catastrophic.

If the hair had a root, then a standard DNA test could be achieved in four or five days, especially if Worthington used his influence to rush it through. For a hair without a root, the more complex type of test, a mitochondrial DNA test, would take at least six to eight weeks and could not possibly be ready yet.

Whatever forensic results they had, if it was Hardy's hair found on the victim, it would prove that he had physical contact with the victim shortly before his death. I knew I was going to have to have a serious conversation with the judge, and soon.

"Hey, you still here?" Becky asked, bringing me out of my thoughts and back to dinner.

"What?" I asked kind of foolishly, before adding, "I'm sorry."

"You're still thinking about the case, aren't you?"

"Yes," I admitted. "It's got me worried. I know in my heart he didn't kill Russell, but how did his hair get on the body?"

"Don't know," Becky said, putting a forkful of potato into her mouth. "Ask him tomorrow. Tonight, eat your dinner and pay attention to me."

"Sounds like a plan," I said, reaching over and putting my hand on hers.

We finished our meal and I made sure to keep my focus on our conversation and our evening together. Becky was very understanding, but I knew better than to poke the bear.

Eddie was disappointed when neither of us ordered dessert. "Are you sure?" he asked. "Tonight I've got tiramisu. Great stuff."

We told him we couldn't eat another bite. Eddie brought the check and I paid it. As we left, Eddie gave me his usual advice, though slightly edited.

"Don't let the you-know-whats get you down, Clubber," he chimed.

He usually said, "Don't let the fuckers get you down," but Eddie was old school and hesitant to swear strongly in front of women. If I had come alone tonight, he would no doubt have cursed enough to make a sailor blush.

As we walked to the car, Becky leaned in and asked, "You-know-whats?"

I whispered the actual expression in her ear. When she heard it, she just said, "Oh," and turned crimson red.

I burst out laughing and pulled her close as we walked.

I drove straight to Becky's house and brought her to the door. She opened it, but turned back to me and put her hand on my chest to stop me from entering.

"Your mind has been elsewhere tonight," she said. "If I invite you in, I want your full attention."

I put my arms around her and pulled her close.

"Yes, ma'am," I said, and kissed her softly.

When the kiss ended, she stared right through my eyes as only she could. Then, she smiled and led me through the door.

She brought me to the couch and asked me to sit. Without a word, she walked to the kitchen. She returned a minute later with two glasses of white wine. She handed me one and sat next to me on the couch.

"I won't be able to see you for a couple of days," she said. "Robert has me working the late afternoon and evening shift."

"The bastard," I said sarcastically.

"No, it's fine," she said seriously. "You need time to handle this case. This isn't just any client."

"That's true," I said, "Hardy is..."

I paused, not exactly sure how to finish the sentence.

"I understand," Becky said.

Then she stood up. "I'll be right back," she announced and walked through her bedroom door, closing it behind her.

I sipped my wine and thought back to my uncompleted sentence. How would I have finished it? He was certainly a mentor and a friend, but that didn't quite cover it. Whatever he was, he was in trouble. I had to find a way to help him.

I had just finished my wine when Becky returned.

"Do I have your attention now?"

I looked up. Becky was standing in the now open bedroom doorway. She was wearing a blue satin chemise. She looked breathtaking.

As I walked toward her in anticipation of a night of bliss, I said, "I assure you. I am fully at attention."

CHAPTER SEVEN

I awoke the next morning to the wonderful smell of bacon. I stood, pulled on my clothes, and staggered out to the kitchen.

Becky was at the stove. She turned as I pulled back the chair to sit down.

"About time you got up," she said cheerily. "Coffee and eggs are up and bacon is almost ready. I was going to just make you an omelet, but while the eggs were cooking, I remembered how much you love bacon."

On the table in front of me was a mug of coffee and a plate with a ham and cheese omelet.

I was not normally a breakfast person. I usually just grabbed coffee and a muffin or maybe a donut at the local store on the way to the office. However, since she had taken the time to cook, and since I wholeheartedly believe it is a crime against everything masculine to turn down bacon, I made an exception.

I was glad I did. I had not realized just how hungry I was until she came over with the pan of bacon just minutes later. I had already finished more than half of the omelet and all of the coffee.

Becky put four strips of bacon on my plate. I got right to work on them.

"Boy, you act like you haven't eaten in weeks," she said.

I swallowed another mouthful of bacon before looking up at her and winking. "I guess I worked up an appetite last night."

She smiled broadly. "Can't argue with that," she replied.

She returned the frying pan to the stove, filled a mug with coffee for herself, and then sat next to me at the table.

"So, what's on your agenda today, Mr. Lawyer?" she asked.

"Well," I said, "I have to meet with Dom. Hopefully, he's been able to find out some of the evidence Worthington has against Hardy. Then, we can start building a defense."

"Good luck with that," she answered. "I'm gonna go back to bed for a while. I have to be at the restaurant by one o'clock and I can expect to get back home around ten-thirty or eleven."

"Good luck with that," I said sarcastically.

I finished eating and offered to help with the dishes. Becky refused my help and ordered me out in a nice but stern way. I gave her a quick kiss and left. Knowing I would not see her for at least two days was certainly a downer, but it was probably for the best. I needed to focus on defending John Hardy and just seeing Becky smile was enough to make me forget everything else.

I drove back to my house. I shaved, showered, and put on a fresh set of clothes. I chose a navy-blue suit with a red silk tie and matching handkerchief.

About ten minutes later, I left and started driving to the office. I had a local radio station playing and was singing along when I realized I was driving right past the County Courthouse. I pulled over and got out. A few feet away was the tree where Gilbert Russell had been found hanging. I had always liked this old tree, but today it had an ominous feel about it, as if it signified death and desolation.

I approached and carefully examined the tree hoping I might find something significant. There was no damage to the branch where Russell had been hanged. None of the bark on the trunk seemed disturbed. Although there were a number of footprints around the tree, there were no signs of a struggle or any indication that Russell had even put up a fight.

Granted, it had been a couple of weeks since the gruesome discovery. It was entirely possible that any such signs had been damaged or obliterated. I made a mental note to look over the police records Dom was bringing. If there had been anything important noted that morning, it should have been documented.

"Well good morning, Counselor," came a familiar voice from behind me.

I turned and saw Larry Watson walking toward me across the grass.

He smiled and said, "Had a feeling I might see you around here."

"Is that so?" I asked.

"Of course," Larry replied, "You're representing Judge Hardy. You have to come to the scene of the crime, right? That's what they always do on the TV shows."

I smiled. "Yes," I offered, "something like that."

"I used to love walking by this tree," Larry continued, "Now, it's hard not to think about finding that dirtbag swinging in the breeze."

"You were the one who found him," I asked, my voice rising in surprise.

"You bet I did," Larry said, "I knew as soon as I saw him hanging there that this was going to be a real shit show. Never dreamed that Judge Hardy would be the one arrested for it though."

I realized this was a fortuitous break. I hadn't seen any police reports yet, but this was a chance to get information directly from an important source. Larry Watson had been the first person at the scene after the killer. Even better, he was retired law enforcement, having served for many years as a guard at the County Jail. He would have noticed anything important.

"Hey, Larry," I asked, "When you came upon the body, was there any indication of a fight or struggle?"

He immediately shook his head. "Not at all," he said, "and there were no marks on the body either."

"Nothing," I asked incredulously.

"Nada," Larry continued. "There were no bruises on his face or cuts on his hands. However, he got up there, it was without any resistance from him."

I paused for a second as my mind raced.

"I'll tell you something else," Larry continued. "There ain't no fucking way John Hardy hanged that piece of shit."

I started to talk, but Larry cut me right off.

"Look here," he said, "Russell weighed about two hundred forty, maybe two hundred fifty pounds, right?"

I nodded, not wanting to stop his flow.

"You tell me then," Watson resumed, "how did an old man like John Hardy take down that fat slob?"

It was a good point. I decided to play devil's advocate for a moment.

"He could have confronted him with a gun and made him come to this very spot." I offered.

Watson laughed derisively. "And how in the hell would John Hardy have lifted all that weight with the rope? You'd need a fucking crane or two or three strong men to lift him up."

I thought for a moment. "He could have forced Russell to walk up a ladder at gun point and tie the noose around his neck. Then kicked out the ladder."

Larry paused briefly before attacking my argument.

"No fucking way. Hardy would not have been strong enough to kick out the ladder. I don't buy it."

I had to admit that Larry had a good point. It seemed highly unlikely that John could have arranged for this execution alone. He certainly could not have lifted Gilbert Russell's weight alone. I doubted a jury would ever believe John Hardy as the lone killer, but any good district attorney (or even a bad one like Worthington) would argue that Hardy did it, but had an accomplice or two.

"Besides," Larry persisted, interrupting my thoughts, "if he had kicked out a ladder, the noise would have been tremendous."

"What do you mean?" I asked. "If the ladder hit the grass, it wouldn't have been that loud."

"It wouldn't have hit the grass," Larry insisted. "He was hanging far enough out on that branch that he was over the pavement of the street, not the grass. The ladder would have hit the concrete and would have been heard."

"Even late at night?" I asked.

"Certainly," Larry chimed. "The police station is down the road. On the night shift, the guys tend to play cards and smoke cigars in the station. They open the windows to let the cigar smoke out so the morning Lieutenant doesn't find clouds of smoke in the building. If that ladder hit the concrete, they would have heard it."

I was impressed. "You sound like you've given this a lot of thought."

"We all have," Larry said proudly. "Everyone at the Courthouse is talking about it, and everyone has their own theory."

"I suppose you have your own theory?"

"You bet your ass," Larry announced.

"Tell me about it," I prompted.

"Well," Larry began, "I think a group of fathers with young girls got together. They found Russell and brought him here at gunpoint. Then, while at least two of them kept him covered, they threw the rope over the branch, tied it around his neck, and hoisted him up."

"Wait a minute," I said holding out my palms to signal Larry not to speak. "You said there were no bruises anywhere on Russell's hands?"

"Not a one," Larry responded, "and I looked carefully."

"His hands and feet weren't tied?" I asked.

"Nope."

The wheels in my head were turning faster and faster. Although the idea of a group of angry men trying to protect their children from a perverted monster made plausible suspects, the lack of any bruises or cuts to the face or hands made the rest of his theory impossible. First, I doubted angry fathers would resist from beating the hell out of a pervert threatening their children.

Second, if they had pulled him up without his hands being tied, Russell would have struggled and there would have been damage to his fingernails as he tried to get his hands under the rope tightening around his neck. He also would have tried to grab the rope above his head and pull himself up.

Third, the idea of this happening in absolute silence seemed far-fetched. A vigilante gang of fathers defending their children would have made more than enough noise for the local police to hear.

"Well," Larry said, "I have to get back to work. Do us all a favor, Connor. Make sure John Hardy gets off. Nobody deserves to go to jail for snuffing out Gilbert Russell. That ain't murder. It's fucking civic improvement."

We shook hands and Larry Watson walked back into the courthouse.

I got into my Cherokee and pulled away, heading toward my office. As I drove, I continued to ponder everything Larry Watson had said. Although his theory of the case had no merit, he was right that this crime was not likely pulled off by John Hardy or any one man. But, how could a group of people have brought Russell to the tree and hanged him without being heard or attracting attention?

Then, I had it. My own theory coalesced in my consciousness as if by magic. One man could not have committed this crime unless that man was Gilbert Russell himself. It all made sense. What if Gilbert Russell had decided to get even with Judge Hardy by committing suicide and framing him for murder? Hardy had made the statement about wanting to see Russell hanged from the nearest tree. All he had to do was pin the note on himself, climb the tree, and hang himself. The obvious suspect would be John Hardy.

My elation lasted only a few seconds when I realized that there was a huge problem. I could almost hear Worthington's annoying voice saying, "If Gilbert Russell killed himself and framed Judge Hardy, how did John Hardy's hair get on the body?" I would have to convince the jury that Russell planted the hair on his own body. Suddenly, my theory had a big hole in it and seemed as bad as Larry's idea.

CHAPTER EIGHT

I arrived at my law office. It was in a small brick and stone two-storey building that had once belonged to a prominent and powerful state senator back in the 1940s. It had been the site of many major political decisions for the county. Ever since then, the building had the nickname of "Headquarters".

I had purchased the building about a year and half previously. I used the first floor for my office and the second floor as an apartment. The place mostly served as office storage space because I almost never stayed there. The office safe was housed in the kitchen area and I always left at least two suits and a pair of shoes in the apartment in case of emergency.

As I pulled into my parking spot around back, I made a mental note to make sure to bring yesterday's suit to the cleaners. I only had one clean emergency suit. It was always a good idea to have at least two.

I walked through the rear entrance. Casey was at her desk as always. She was dressed in a dark-green, short-sleeve blouse and gray slacks. Just barely appearing from under her sleeves were her colorful tattoos on her shoulders and upper arms: flowers on the right and a dog on the left. Her dark-brown hair was pulled back in a ponytail, which was slightly unusual. She usually wore it loose about her shoulders.

As I walked past her, she handed me a mug full of coffee and my printed-out daily schedule. She always had both of these ready for me like clockwork.

I thanked her and continued into my office. I sat in my oversized leather chair, sipped my coffee, and began to review my schedule.

At 10:00am, the schedule just read, "Mr. Wonderful". That of course referred to Dom. The rest of my schedule was empty. I found this odd, as I knew I had at least two more clients scheduled for the afternoon.

I looked toward my office door to shout for Casey. I was about to utter the first syllable when I realized she was already in the doorway.

"I called your two afternoon appointments and postponed them until next week," she offered. "I figured once Mr. Wonderful arrived, you would have me move them anyway. So, I just took care of it."

Though I would have preferred if she had checked with me first, I decided not to say anything. The truth was that I had already considered asking her to reschedule both appointments anyway.

"When Dom gets here, bring him right in," I said, before taking another sip of my coffee.

"No problem," Casey replied, heading for the door. "I'll bring him right in. I just hope his inflated ego can fit through the door."

I smiled and shook my head as she left. It just wasn't a day at the office without Casey taking a shot at Dom, and vice versa.

Their relationship is very complicated. Both relish the opportunity to hurl insults at the other. Their sparring often gets to the to the point of screaming, shouting, and verbal warfare.

Any reasonable person witnessing their back and forth would think they hated each other. Yet deep down, they care very deeply for one another, in a father–daughter or uncle–niece kind of way. When Casey had nearly been killed just a few months ago by the Rockfield Strangler, tough and hard-nosed detective Dom Bryce wept and pleaded with her to hang on. It had been the only time I had ever seen the man cry.

"Oh, by the way," Casey hollered from her desk, "this morning's newspaper is on your desk."

This was rather odd. Coffee and my schedule were always there first thing in the morning. I could not recall Casey ever bringing me a newspaper.

I thanked her and picked up the paper. The headline was in big bold print.

JUDGE HARDY ARRESTED FOR MURDER OF LOCAL CHILD KILLER

No bias there, I thought.

Beneath the headline was a color picture of Judge Hardy from one of his previous election campaigns. He had on his biggest and best "vote for me" smile.

The article itself was fairly benign. It mentioned some of the comments made by Worthington and me at the hearing, and praised Judge Marino for maintaining order. I snickered slightly to myself when I read that.

The story was just getting to the point where we argued about bail, when it stopped abruptly with an instruction to turn to page five. I turned quickly to continue reading. When I got to page five, I almost fell out of my chair.

At the very top of the page was a photograph of me. It was captioned:

Local Attorney Connor Phelan Arrives in Court to Fight for his Client.

That was fine, except the picture had been taken just after I'd walked through the court's metal detectors. I was dressed in my judo gi and black belt. One of the reporters had obviously seen me, recognized me, and snapped a quick picture.

"Oh, shit," I said aloud.

Almost immediately, I heard Casey howling with laughter from the other room.

"Connor Phelan fights for his clients!" she shouted through her laughter, barely able to get the words out. "Hiiii yah!!" she yelled, making a karate sound similar to *Miss Piggy* from *The Muppets*, before breaking out in laughter again.

I walked to my office door. I could see Casey seated at her desk. She was leaning back in her chair and laughing so hard that tears were running down her face.

"Very funny," I said. I closed the door and returned to my desk.

Though it was difficult to get past the picture of me, I managed to read the remainder of the article. It covered the rest of the court appearance accurately. It finished with an ominous statement. "If convicted, Judge Hardy faces a potential life sentence."

I folded up the paper and sat back in my own chair to think. A life sentence for a man who didn't do it. But, I thought, they have his DNA on the deceased's body. My own doubts about his guilt or innocence resumed battling in my head. My heart told me that John Hardy would never commit a blatant and brutal murder. In my head, however, thoughts about DNA and Hardy's words in court that Russell deserved to be hanged swirled endlessly.

I was still lost in thought when a knock at the door brought me sharply back to reality.

"Come in," I said.

The door opened and Casey peeked in.

"Finished laughing?" I asked sarcastically.

"Never," she replied, "but there's an older lady here who insists on speaking with you. She won't take no for an answer."

"Okay," I said, "Bring her in."

Casey opened the door fully and turned toward the waiting room.

"Okay, ma'am," she said. "You can come in."

Hearing Casey call someone "ma'am" was unusual. She could certainly be polite, but rarely in such a formal way. I understood immediately why she was being so polite when I saw who the mystery woman was. I stood immediately out of respect.

Mrs. Harriet Edwards walked into my office. Mrs. Edwards had been my second-grade teacher. In fact, she had been the second-grade teacher for just about everyone who grew up in Rockfield.

Harriet Edwards had started teaching second grade at Abraham Lincoln Elementary School in 1952 at the age of twenty-five. She continued at that same school for sixty years, retiring in 2012 at the age of eighty-five.

Every kid who had ever walked into her classroom loved her, respected her, and feared her. She was a wonderful teacher who went out of her way to get to know each of her students. She was always very nice, but also stern and strict. She did not tolerate misbehavior. She almost never sent a child to the principal's office. She handled matters of discipline herself.

Once her class understood that following Mrs. Edwards' rules was more than just a good idea, things went smoothly. They learned their lessons and became intensely loyal to their teacher. She would bring in cookies and put on puppet shows. She knitted her own puppets and provided each one with its own voice and character. Her shows were always fun, but at the same time taught something.

When she retired, her going away party had to be held in one of the city parks as there was no reception hall anywhere in the county big enough for all the people who insisted on attending. Hundreds and hundreds of people showed up. Local politicians were green with envy at the turnout. I doubt even Judge Hardy himself could have brought in such a crowd.

"Mrs. Edwards, it's wonderful to see you," I said. "Please come in and have a seat."

"Thank you, Mr. Phelan," she said, in the same kind but commanding voice I remembered.

She was wearing a lavender sweater made of wool. I was certain she had knitted it herself. Her hair was completely white and cut in a short pixie-style cut. Although she still seemed young for her age, she now walked with a cane. She only leaned on it slightly and she got to the chair in front of my desk rather quickly.

I sat back in my chair.

"What can I do for you, Mrs. Edwards?" I asked.

"I need your help," she answered with an emphasis on the last word.

I expected she was going to ask me about a will or estate planning. I could not have been more wrong.

"I have a problem with some hoodlums," she announced.

"Hoodlums?" I asked.

"Yes," she said with a strong nod of her head. "I need your help with some hoodlums and hooligans."

I found her choice of vocabulary to be very amusing, but I fought fiercely to keep from smiling.

"Are these hooligans bothering you, Mrs. Edwards."

"Yes," she said strongly. "They keep coming on my land every single night just before dark without permission. Then, they go over to an old shed near the back of my property. My sons, Ronnie and Jimmy, used to play in that shed. They called it their fort."

Now, I smiled, remembering my time as a child. Every boy had to have his own fort. It was just required. Mine had been a tiny little shack my dad had built for me out of two by fours and some plywood. I spent many good hours in that fort.

"Mr. Phelan," she said firmly, "I don't want them there. If they get hurt, I'm the one who will be responsible."

"Have you called the police?" I asked.

"Yes, but they don't take it seriously," she said. "They think I'm just being a grouchy old lady."

"Well," I said, "I don't think you're grouchy."

"I can be," she insisted. "I'm sure you remember that."

"Yes, ma'am," I replied, "but you were never grouchy. You were in charge, but never unkind."

"Well, when you get to be an old woman," she continued, "you find out that sometimes being crabby is the only way you can get young people to listen to you."

"I suppose," I conceded, "but I'm sure that—"

"I tried talking with those young men," she interrupted, "but it did no good. They called me names and told me to shut up."

That caught my attention, and I felt my anger begin to grow.

"What did they say exactly?" I asked in a tone that made it clear I wanted a direct answer.

"I told them they did not have my permission to be on my property," she said. Then the biggest of the three said...well..."

She paused and was obviously uncomfortable.

"What's the matter, Mrs. Edwards?" I asked.

"Well, he used words that I don't think a lady should use," she answered.

"I understand that," I said sympathetically. "Maybe for the improper words, you just use the first letter of the word. I think I'll be able to figure it out."

"Fine," she said. She took a deep breath and steadied herself. "The big one said. 'Shut the f up, you old bat, before I come up there and beat the s out of you.'"

Her eyes were glassy and her face was red with embarrassment even with just using f and s. My face was probably red too. I was livid. The idea of some punk talking that way to Mrs. Edwards made my blood boil.

"I will take your case, Mrs. Edwards," I said intently. "I will make sure they leave you alone."

"How are you going to do that?" she asked.

I knew exactly how I was going to do it, but felt it better that Mrs. Edwards not know the details.

"Just leave it to me, ma'am," I said. "I'll handle it."

"Very well," she replied curtly. "But, before I leave, what about your fee?"

"That's okay, Mrs. Edwards," I said, "there's no need for..."

"Oh, no," she said defiantly, pounding her fist on my desk. "If I am retaining your services, I expect to pay my bill."

I didn't want to take her money, but knew I couldn't win an argument with her. She was a proud and stubborn woman. Then, I had an epiphany and knew how I could satisfy both of our concerns.

"Fine, Mrs. Edwards," I said, "but my attorney fee will not be for money."

She looked at me quizzically. "I'm not sure I understand."

I smiled. "A fee is something of value given in exchange for services, right?"

"Yes," she answered almost suspiciously.

"Do you still bake, Mrs. Edwards?"

"I sure do," she answered with a cheeky grin.

"Well then," I said, "I will take your case and deal with your hooligans and hoodlums in return for a plate of your famous cookies."

"As I recall," she said, "your favorite was my special coconut chocolate chip."

"Yes, ma'am."

She stood up and said, "We have a deal."

I stood as well and escorted her through the door and into the waiting room.

Casey was at her desk and Dom Bryce was seated in one of waiting-room chairs. When he saw Harriet Edwards, he immediately stood up and took off his cowboy hat.

"Good morning, Mrs. Edwards," he said clumsily. "Uh, nice to see you, ma'am."

"And good morning to you, Mr. Bryce," she answered sternly. "It's nice to see you still remember your manners, young man."

"You taught me well, Mrs. Edwards," he replied. Dom seemed very nervous in her presence.

"You were a very rude young man, Mr. Bryce," she said matter-of-factly. "That is until I put you over my knee and pounded some sense into you."

"Yes, ma'am," Dom answered, his face reddening.

Casey's face lit up like she had just seen all of her gifts under the Christmas tree.

"Mr. Phelan, I'm sure you and Mr. Bryce have important business to discuss," she chimed happily. "Why don't I escort Mrs. Edwards to her car?"

Dom rolled his eyes in frustration as I held back laughter.

"That okay with you, Mrs. Edwards?" I asked.

"That would be just fine, dear" she said

"I will be at your house this evening just before dark to speak with you about your case," I said.

"I will see you then, Mr. Phelan," she replied.

Casey offered her arm and Harriet Edwards took it. As they went past Dom, Casey gave him a triumphant smile. Dom looked like he wanted to strangle her.

As the ladies walked out the door, I heard Casey say, "So, Mrs. Edwards, tell me again how you taught Mr. Bryce about manners."

CHAPTER NINE

I invited Dom into my office. He came in grumbling under his breath.

"That darn girl just burns me," he said. "I'm sure I'll never hear the end of that."

"Oh, relax," I said, trying to calm him down. "That was over fifty years ago."

"I know," he grunted, "but that woman is plain nosy."

Dom kept mumbling as he sat in the chair our former teacher was using just moments ago.

Dom was dressed in a red button-down shirt and blue jeans. His belt had a very large buckle that expressed in no uncertain terms his support of the individual right to bear arms. If the buckle didn't tell the story, the pearl-handled Colt 45 revolver in his hip holster definitely did. To finish his ensemble, he wore a brown cowboy hat and matching leather boots; just a cliché of the old west.

As I sat in my chair, Dom tossed a manila folder he had been carrying. It landed on the desk directly in front of me. As I picked it up, Dom leaned back in his chair and put his feet on the end of my desk.

"I assume this is the police file on John Hardy?" I asked.

"Almost all of it," Dom replied.

"Almost?" I asked suspiciously. "What's missing?"

"Not sure," he answered. "The detective who got it for me said a few reports had been removed and were only to be found in the district attorney's file."

That caught my attention. It told me right away that there was something important that D.A. Worthington wanted kept quiet.

"What were those reports?" I asked as I started looking at the file.

"No, idea," Dom said. "My buddy didn't know. He just knew that two or three reports were removed from the file. He was none too happy about it either."

"Any other big surprises in here I should know about?" I asked sarcastically.

"I haven't had time to read it, Connor," replied Dom. "I got it about thirty minutes ago and I came right over."

The file was divided into numerous folders. I dug through them until I found one marked "DNA". Inside was a report from the State Police Lab. I read through the report quickly and felt my heart sink.

The laboratory analysis showed that DNA had been obtained from one of the four hairs found on Gilbert Russell's body. The other hairs did not have roots. A comparison was made against a DNA sample given voluntarily by Judge Hardy. They were a perfect match.

Worthington had not been lying or bluffing. They did indeed have Hardy's DNA on the body of Gilbert Russell. It was not just solid evidence. It was incriminating and devastating evidence.

I set the DNA folder aside in disgust and started rooting through the rest of the file. The next folder I opened was labeled

"Autopsy". Inside was a copy of the official autopsy report on Gilbert Russell. I placed the rest of the file down and started reviewing the coroner's report.

When Dom saw what I was reading, he laughed. "Pretty clear what the cause of death is. He was fucking hanged," he snorted.

I skimmed the report looking for the official cause of death. When I found it, it was not what I expected.

"Not so clear at all, boss," I said.

Dom's feet came off my desk and he sat straight up.

"What do you have?" he asked.

"There are two causes of death," I announced, feeling the shock of my own words. "The first is death by ligature strangulation, but the second is cardiac arrest caused by extremely high levels of Ketamine and alcohol."

Dom whistled in surprise. "He fell into the k-hole," he said.

"What the fuck is a k-hole?" I asked. "Ketamine is horse tranquilizer, isn't it?"

"Yeah, it is," Dom answered, "but it's also a common drug in the club scene. Kids take it because when you have a strong enough dose, the high is so intense that you lose almost complete contact with the world. They sometimes can't even speak. It's not coma, but it's more than feeling intoxicated. I've heard users say the sensation is like floating out of their bodies or a near-death experience. Complete dissociation. Kids call it falling down the k-hole."

I sat back in my chair and let Dom's words sink in. Just the thought of it made me feel nauseous. Why would anyone want to do such a thing?

Yet, what scared me more than that thought was the partial understanding of it all. After my wife died, I had done everything I could to shut my life down and not face the painful reality of the world.

I'd had everything I had ever wanted. I could not have been happier. Then, in the blink of an eye, I'd lost it all.

I'd met my wife-to-be, Melissa Cooper, when she'd been prosecuting sex crimes as an assistant district attorney. She was one of the most beautiful women I had ever seen. In less than six months, we were married. Two months after that, Melissa was pregnant with our son. I'd been in court arguing a bail application when one of the bailiffs pulled me aside to tell me that Melissa had been brought to Linton Memorial Hospital. He had no details other than that it was very serious, and I needed to get to the hospital right away. I had driven as fast as I could and was met at the entrance of the Emergency Room by one of the doctors. I went completely numb as the doctor explained that my wife had a previously undetected brain aneurysm that had ruptured, killing her almost instantly. She was alone when she collapsed. Melissa and my unborn son, whom we had decided to name Connor Jr., were dead before help could even arrive.

After Melissa and my unborn son died, I no longer had any fire left in me. I quit my job within a month and took a job with a large firm in New York City. Though I continued to be a lawyer, I focused my efforts on civil law and representing injured people. My life as a prosecutor was effectively over. Hell, I hadn't really been living. I'd just been going through the motions.

Might I have considered falling down the k-hole if I had known about it back then? The idea made the hairs on my arm stand on end.

After a moment, I brought my concentration back to the report.

"It says Russell was also drunk," I continued. "He was point two four on the blood test. You put that with high levels of Ketamine—"

"And he's all kinds of fucked up," Dom said, finishing my sentence.

So, not likely he was going to be able fight off his killer," I suggested.

Dom laughed derisively. "Fight him off? That scumbag was so far down the hole, he was probably unconscious when he was hanged. Might have died even if he wasn't strung up."

I started to read the rest of the report. I was only a few paragraphs in when Dom spoke again.

"Too bad John didn't wait a few hours before he hanged him," he said. "Son of a bitch might have died on his own."

I slammed my hands down on my desk. "John Hardy did not kill Gilbert Russell," I shouted.

Dom put up his hands in mock surrender. "Take it easy, buddy," he said, "I was just joking around."

I didn't say anything for a moment. My sudden burst of anger even surprised me. Perhaps the constant war between my head and heart was taking its toll. My gut told me that Hardy was not a murderer. Yet, my brain couldn't seem to let go of the doubt.

"Sorry," I finally said. "Guess this case is getting to me."

Dom said nothing and I went back to reading the coroner's report. As I was reading through the examination findings, a thought occurred to me.

"Dom, how is Ketamine taken? Is it snorted? Smoked?"

"Both," he answered, "plus it can be swallowed or injected like heroin."

"If Russell were a user, how would he likely take it?" I asked. "Quickest way, right?"

"Probably," Dom replied. "Injection gets you there first."

I started checking the coroner's report looking for any physical indications of Ketamine use, other than the blood test.

Nothing was found in the nose, so that likely ruled out snorting. No evidence of track marks on the arms.

When I found what I was looking for, I couldn't help but express my surprise.

"Holy shit," I said.

"What is it?" Dom asked.

"Russell didn't take Ketamine," I said.

"What are you talking about?" Dom demanded. "It's in his blood stream."

"You don't understand," I said. "Russell didn't take the drug intentionally. It was forced on him."

"How do you know that?" Dom pressed.

"Coroner found a wound on the left side of Russell's behind with traces of Ketamine on the outside of the wound," I said. "Someone shot him with a tranquilizer dart."

"He was shot in the ass with a tranq dart?" Dom asked, bursting into laughter.

"No question about it," I replied. "By the time he was hanged, he must have been completely out of it. That explains why there are no other significant wounds on the body."

"Other wounds?" Dom asked.

"Think of it this way," I said. "If someone was trying to hang me from a tree, there would have been multiple cuts and bruises on my knuckles from me punching the son of a bitch. Gilbert had none. Tells me that the killer shot Russell with the tranquilizer dart and took him without a fight."

When Dom started chuckling again, I shot him a dirty look.

"You going to laugh every time I mention him getting shot in the ass?" I asked.

"Probably," Dom answered, continuing to snicker.

I shook my head in frustration and went back to reviewing the police file. There was a thicker folder entitled "Witness statements".

I opened it and found written statements from Al and Jamie Lawson, the dead girl's parents. They both claimed to have been home all night on the evening of Russell's murder. They basically gave alibis for each other. Convenient, I thought to myself.

There were other statements from people including from Larry Watson, the man who found the body. I read his affidavit carefully, but it offered nothing that I did not already know.

What did catch my attention was a signed statement from Joey Greene, a bartender at the Rusty Bull. The Rusty Bull is a small dive bar located a few miles outside of town. Located in a very rural area, it was known for being a place where people went to drink hardcore and be left alone.

Gilbert Russell had been drinking for several hours on the night of his death, and Greene had seen him. Just before 2:30am, Greene had told Russell he had to leave because he was closing. Apparently, Gilbert became hostile when Greene had refused to give him back his car keys.

According to Joey's statement, he watched Russell leave the bar to make sure he didn't have another set of keys for his car. Russell walked out of the parking lot and started down County Route 304.

Now the statement got really interesting. Greene reported seeing a rusty pickup truck stop by Gilbert Russell. Russell had spoken to the driver and then walked around back and started climbing into the rear tailgate. The drunken Russell was most of the way into the back when the driver backed up quickly, kicking dust into the air. Russell flopped into the bed of the truck clumsily. Then, after delaying for about twenty or thirty seconds, the driver had shifted into drive and taken off at a high rate of speed. Greene never saw the driver.

The final paragraph of the statement really grabbed me. It said:

> The police showed me a still picture
> taken from a DVD. The truck in that
> picture looks like the one I saw Gilbert
> Russell climb into, but I cannot be
> sure.

"DVD?" I said aloud.

"Oh, that," Dom said immediately. "They pulled some video footage from a security camera in front of a store near the courthouse. The detective said it shows an old truck driving away from where the scumbag was hanged. No plates or clear footage of the killer though."

I immediately started searching for the DVD and I found it in the very last folder, along with a copy of the still photo that Greene mentioned. I knew it was the same because whomever the detective was who'd taken the statement had the good sense to have Greene initial the picture.

I examined the picture carefully. It showed the passenger front of what looked like a 1979 Ford Ranger pick-up. It had once been metallic silver, but now was old, dirty, and very rusty. The bed of the truck could not be seen as most of it was obscured by a large tree. I realized quickly that this was the same tree that Gilbert Russell had been hanging from when found.

Because the picture had been taken in the dead of night, deciphering much detail from the image was difficult. I knew from memory of the location that there was a streetlight just down the road from that tree. It was the only light on that side of the street. Also, the camera that shot the video hadn't been installed for the purposes of watching that tree, so the footage had been recorded at a terrible angle. If that wasn't bad enough, the photo was somewhat blurry.

There was enough resolution to tell what kind of truck it

was. Although the passenger window was visible, nothing could be seen inside the truck.

When I was satisfied that I had seen everything from the picture that there was to see, I opened the DVD case. I took the DVD to the credenza on the other side of my office. I have a TV/DVD combo there that I keep for evidence viewing. I also use it for news broadcasts when I have a tough case and for watching baseball games when I am working late or over a weekend.

I popped in the DVD, grabbed the remote, and hit play. The grainy footage was tough to see, as the left side of the picture was dark and blocked by the old tree. The right side was brighter from the streetlight and much easier to see.

After a few seconds, the Ford Ranger pulled up and parked. The truck shook slightly, probably from the driver's door opening and closing. I tried as hard as I could to see if I could make out a driver. No luck.

I saw the truck shake again and surmised that the driver had opened the tailgate and climbed on. Maybe thirty seconds later, the truck shook again, though more forcefully. The driver must have slammed the tailgate shut. I again saw movement consistent with the driver's door opening and closing.

I was very frustrated that nothing of the driver could be seen at all. It was stupid, perhaps, to expect a clear picture of the killer. That only happened in the movies. Still, I like those old movies and so I had to try. Then, the lights of the truck flared to life and it sped off out of the view of the camera.

I decided to rewind the video and watch it again. This time, I watched it in slow motion. Everything was exactly the same except painfully slower. Near the end of the video, something caught my eye as the truck drove away. It was a sudden movement from behind the tree.

I rewound again. This time, I watched only the area where I

saw the unknown movement. As the truck started forward, I realized with sickening horror what had probably happened.

The killer must have tied the rope around Russell's neck as he lay in the bed of the truck. When the truck went forward and the rope went taut, Russell's body yanked upward. As the truck continued forward, the closed tailgate struck the body on its way up and caused Russell's legs to flop in the air. In the video, in slow motion, I could see part of Russell's white sneakers for just a second after his body hit the tailgate. They were only visible for a split second before the rope around his neck pulled Russell to his death.

The sequence of events now seemed pretty clear. The killer picked up Gilbert Russell near the Rusty Bull and offered him a ride. When Gilbert clumsily climbed most of the way into the truck bed, the killer slammed the car in reverse, causing Russell to fall the rest of the way in.

The killer stopped briefly. I guessed that this was when he shot Russell with the tranquilizer dart though the rear cab window. Then, after making sure he was secure, the killer drove off to the courthouse to complete the execution. He drove under the tree, got out and into the truck bed. He tied the rope around Russell's neck. He might have tied it to the tree then, though I doubted it. It had happened too quickly. This told me that the killer most likely tied the rope to the tree branch before he picked up Russell.

Once the rope was secure around Gilbert Russell's neck, he drove the truck out from under Russell and completed the hanging. Gruesome, but effective, I thought.

I began to feel nauseous as I realized that not only was it possible for this crime to be committed by one person, the DVD proved it had in fact been done by one person. As if that wasn't bad enough, the lack of defensive wounds was now explained. Russell had not fought back because he had been unconscious.

My defense theories were down in the k-hole with Gilbert Russell.

I looked over at Dom. "Well, we now know exactly how the killing took place," I said.

Dom nodded. Then he said, "True, but the only evidence to the killer's identity is the DNA, and that points right at John Hardy."

I sighed almost reflexively. He was right. The DNA was the entire case. It would prove to a jury that Hardy was the man who killed Gilbert Russell.

It was very frustrating. District Attorney Worthington now had Hardy's head in the noose, and I had absolutely no idea how I was going to save him.

CHAPTER TEN

After Dom left. I spent the next two hours reading and re-reading the file. Soon, I had every document committed to memory. There was no other evidence against Hardy. The entire case was his threat and the DNA. If I could somehow either explain the presence of DNA at the scene or prove the lab test inaccurate, the entire case would collapse. If wishes were horses, beggars would ride.

Yet, something about the case file bothered me. There were documents that had been removed from the file by the District Attorney's Office. I wondered what they might be and why they had been removed.

It was clear that Worthington did not want me to see them or learn of their contents until the trial itself. He had to know that Dom would have been able to see the file and get me a copy. What could be so damn important that it had to be hidden from me?

More than that was the feeling I could not shake, that I had missed something. I felt like I had assembled a puzzle but had a missing piece. Worse, I didn't know what the piece looked like. I was certain that it was something simple, something I should have noticed. Try as I might, the answer kept eluding me.

I was still considering the mystery when my phone intercom buzzed. I quickly pressed the button.

"Yes, Casey, what is it?" I asked.

"Miss Bollenbacher to see you, Connor," Casey announced.

"Send her in," I replied, as I started putting the folders back into the manila envelope.

I had only just gotten the envelope closed when my office door opened and Ethel Bollenbacher walked in. She was dressed in a dark gray coat. It was unbuttoned, revealing a beige turtleneck sweater underneath. Her hair was pulled tightly into a bun.

"Good afternoon, Mr. Phelan," she said curtly. "May I sit down?"

"Of course," I said, immediately remembering my manners and standing up.

She quietly walked over and sat down. I resumed my seat and waited for her to speak.

"I stopped by to see if you have any updates on Judge Hardy's case," she announced.

"Well, I am investigating the evidence against John," I said. "His preliminary hearing is in two days and I am—"

"Mr. Phelan," Ethel interrupted, "Allow me to explain what I want to know. I want to know the nature of the evidence against Judge Hardy. I also want to know what kind of defense you are going to offer."

"What I can tell you is that the district attorney has DNA evidence linking John to the crime scene," I said.

She raised an eyebrow in surprise. "How do you plan to counter that?" she asked.

I didn't reply right away. I just stared at her as I considered my response.

'What is your defense, Mr. Phelan?" she asked again in a rather demanding tone.

"Miss Bollenbacher," I replied, as tactfully as I could, "you have to understand that I am limited as to what I can tell you."

"Perhaps you have forgotten," she pressed, "that I am the person who paid your initial retainer. I am therefore entitled to know what I am getting for my money."

"Yes, ma'am, you did pay my initial fee," I answered. "What you are receiving for your money is me defending John Hardy."

She opened her mouth to speak, but I raised a finger to signal her to stop, and kept talking.

"I understand that you want more information about the case," I continued. "But my client is John Hardy. Whatever defense we choose to present is between the judge and myself. I cannot discuss the details of that defense, as it is protected by attorney–client privilege. I hope you can appreciate that."

She again opened her mouth to speak, but seemed to reconsider whatever she was planning to say. Then, she stood.

"Very well, Mr. Phelan," she said sternly. "I trust that you *will* keep me apprised of all things that are *not* privileged?"

Her words were phrased as a question, but were clearly intended as a command.

"Yes, ma'am," I replied politely as I stood.

"Thank you," Ethel said.

Then, without another word, she turned and walked out of the office.

A few seconds later, Casey walked into the office carrying two cups of coffee. She handed me one of the mugs and sat down.

"Old Iron Girdle didn't look very happy," she said.

"Well, since she paid the initial retainer, she feels she is entitled to be a part of the defense team," I replied, before taking a sip of my coffee.

"Wish I could have seen the look on her face when you told her no," she said, laughing slightly as she did. "Must have been priceless."

I smiled in spite of myself. "Let's just say she was less than pleased," I offered.

Casey smiled and took a big gulp from her coffee. Then, she stood and headed for the door. She looked back when she was in the doorway.

"She's going to be a real pain in the ass about this case," she said. "She will be back."

When I didn't reply, she asked, "How you going to handle her?"

"I'll sic you on her," I said with a smile.

Casey laughed. As she turned to leave, she said, "Just say the word, Connor. She won't know what hit her."

I laughed to myself. Old Iron Girdle wouldn't stand a chance, I thought.

About an hour later, I decided to go home. I grabbed the manila envelope Dom had brought me and asked Casey to lock up. I hopped in the car and drove off.

The entire way to my house, I was consumed with thoughts of the DNA evidence. If Hardy was innocent, how the hell did his hair get to the crime scene? I considered possibly the court appearance from the day before Russell's death. That didn't make sense. Hardy had been on the bench and never got close to him.

Try as I might, I could not think of an innocent explanation for Hardy's hair being on Russell's corpse.

When I got home, I tossed the manila envelope on my kitchen counter. I decided to take a break from the case and see about supper. I had worked straight through lunch and was starving. I opened my freezer and found two frozen dinners.

One was Salisbury steak and looked awful. The second was meat loaf and looked even worse.

I closed the freezer and opened the refrigerator. Right on top were two beers. That was a good start. There wasn't much else, except for a plastic container on the bottom shelf I had never seen before. There was a post-it note on top.

I took the container out and read the note. It was in Becky's very neat handwriting. It read:

I made you some decent food. Put it on a plate and heat in the microwave.
Do NOT put my plastic Tupperware in the microwave and please don't eat those horrible frozen dinners in your freezer. They look repulsive.
Love, Becky.

I removed the lid. Inside were homemade sausage and peppers. It looked and smelled so good, I thought I might cry. I didn't, but thought I might have if I had eaten the frozen meatloaf instead. I made a mental note to buy something for Becky. I wasn't sure what I would buy her, but I knew one thing never to do—cook for her. She deserved better.

After my dinner was hot, I took it and my beers to the dining room. As I ate, I again read through the file, hoping to find something I had missed all the other times I read it.

When I finished my meal and my beers, I had still not solved the riddle. So, I brought my plate and silverware over to the sink. I washed them along with Becky's Tupperware. The entire time, my mind kept going over and over the case file. What had I missed?

How did those hairs get on the corpse? Suddenly, almost as if my brain was struck by lightning, I realized what I had missed. Hairs had been found on the corpse, but there was no mention of when, where, or by whom. All of the reports offered the conclusion that the hairs had been found on the corpse, but there were no reports detailing where they had been found on the corpse or who had found them.

I could not believe I had been so stupid. I had been so focused on the DNA match with Hardy, I had forgotten to consider these additional details. There should have been a report detailing the discovery of the hairs and explaining who found them and when. The documents I had read all started with the hairs being reviewed at the lab. Who brought them there?

Obviously, these were the reports that had been removed by the District Attorney's Office. But why? Why did Worthington not want anyone to know where the hairs were found? What difference would it make if they had been found on Russell's shirt or pants?

Part of me wanted to go straight to Worthington's office and demand to see the reports. I knew that would be a waste of time. Although New York law had recently been amended to require prosecutors to turn over just about all of their evidence, the prosecutor had fifteen days from arraignment to do so. The preliminary hearing was in two days and I could not force anything in time. Worthington would just tell me to pound salt.

I needed another approach. I had my answer right away. Worthington would never give me anything, but perhaps someone in his office would.

I got my cell phone and called Roger "Bills" Billingsley, Worthington's Chief Investigator. Bills had worked as an investigator with the district attorney's office for many years. After retiring from the Rockville Police Department, he was hired by then District Attorney John Hardy. After Hardy became county court judge, Bills stayed on with J. Robert Worthington.

Bills was highly respected and known as a man who simply didn't lie. If there was chicanery involved in this case, Bills would never stand for it.

He answered on the second ring.

"Hey old man," I said, "Ain't you retired yet?"

"I'm still young enough to whip your butt, boy," he replied jovially.

"I don't doubt it, Bills." I said.

"So, why am I being honored with your phone call, Connor," Bills continued, getting right to the point.

"I need to ask you about the Hardy case," I said.

"Let me stop you right there," Bills interrupted. "I'm not on that case. Worthington thinks I'm too close with Hardy. I know only what's in the newspapers."

"I understand that, but I really need a favor, old man."

Bills paused for a moment, obviously considering my words. Finally, after what seemed like forever, he said, "I won't get you inside information about the evidence, if that's what you're looking for."

"I'm not asking for anything like that, Bills," I said. "I was able to get a look at the police file, but there are documents that Worthington had removed."

"Removed?" Bills asked. "Why the hell would he do that?"

"I'm not sure why," I said, "but it is pretty clear that it has to do with the hairs found on Russell's body. There are no reports about who found them, what part of the body they were found on, or when they were found."

"Are you bullshitting me?" Bills asked suspiciously.

"Bills, you know I've always been straight with you," I said. "There are no reports. There isn't even a report showing who took the hairs to the lab."

"That is damn peculiar," Bills said, "but I can't just root

through files and give evidence to defense attorneys. Worthington would have me up on charges if he caught me.

I thought for a minute. I needed the information, but didn't want Bills to risk his pension. Then, I had an idea.

"Tell you what, Bills," I offered, "take a look at the file. If you look at those reports and don't see anything that looks wrong or out of line, then that's the end of it. But, if you see something that seems... shall we say... unethical?"

"I get your meaning, Connor," said Bills. "You're about as subtle as an atomic bomb."

We both laughed.

"All right, Connor," said Bills in a voice that invited no discussion, "I'll take a look. If I see something that ain't kosher, I'll contact you. Otherwise, this discussion never happened. Capeesh?"

"Capeesh," I responded.

I knew I could always count on Bills. He would always do whatever he thought was honorable. Too bad there aren't more people like him in this world, I thought.

CHAPTER ELEVEN

After I got off the phone with Bills, I changed out of my suit and into jeans and an old, dark, flannel shirt. I also put on sneakers and grabbed a light jacket. I had to go to Mrs. Edwards' house and a suit just wasn't the right attire for the job.

Then, I called Mr. Ito and asked him if he could cover the Tuesday judo class. I explained to him that I was going to confront the punks pestering Mrs. Edwards. He asked if I needed his help.

When I explained to him that I could handle it, and that he could best help me by covering the class, he agreed, but seemed almost disappointed. I thanked him and hung up.

I left the house, jumped into my Cherokee and, about fifteen minutes later, arrived at her home. I parked around the corner and walked to the front door. I figured if the hooligans, as she called them, saw my car, they might go elsewhere. I intended to make this a one-night investigation and solution.

Mrs. Edwards answered the door right away.

"Good evening, Mr. Phelan," she said cheerily. "Please, come in."

I walked inside and she escorted me into her kitchen at the

back of the house. The kitchen was immaculate, though it was styled in the seventies and had never been changed. The floor was aged linoleum. The counter tops were yellow, but the cabinets above and below them were reddish-brown. Above the upper cabinets, the walls were covered by white wallpaper with designs of fruit and vines. The appliances were avocado green. It looked like a kitchen with warm autumn tones out of a Sears Roebuck catalog from 1975.

Mrs. Edwards asked me to sit at the kitchen table and I obliged. Moments later, she brought over tea and biscuits before sitting at the far end of the table.

"Please have some tea," she said. "The hoodlums should be here pretty soon."

I smiled and helped myself to some biscuits. They were light, flaky, and delicious.

I asked Mrs. Edwards what she had been doing with herself since she retired. She smiled warmly and began talking about a few vacations she had taken. Though she was making an effort to be a good host, it was obvious to me that she was edgy and nervous. I hadn't really noticed that when she was in my office. She had seemed just like my old teacher, albeit with gray hair. Now, she was a nervous old woman.

I understood that the punks (or hoodlums and hooligans as she called them) were not just an annoyance to her. Mrs. Edwards was legitimately frightened of them. I decided then and there that this would be the final night they frightened her.

I was on my second cup of tea with milk and honey when Mrs. Edwards stood up suddenly and the color drained from her face. She had tried to keep up a brave front. Now, there was terror in her eyes.

"There they are," she said, her voice quivering.

I looked out and saw two boys walking nonchalantly across her backyard. They looked to be about seventeen or eighteen years old. Both were white and about average height and build. The taller of the two was wearing a dark jacket and a Yankees baseball cap. The other was wearing a light-colored coat and no hat.

I didn't find them particularly intimidating, but I'm not a ninety-three-year-old woman who lives alone.

"Where do they usually go?" I asked.

"To the shed near the back of the yard," she said pointing.

I looked where she pointed and saw a small barn. It was very old and the boys were heading straight for it.

I went through the back door and on to the rear porch. Mrs. Edwards followed me.

"Maybe you should wait inside, Mrs. Edwards," I said.

"No," she said defiantly. "This is my home and I want them gone."

I knew she wouldn't take no for an answer. So, I said, "Fine, but stay on the porch."

She nodded.

I went down the porch steps and started walking quickly toward the boys. I was within ten to fifteen feet of them when Mrs. Edwards suddenly shouted out, "You hooligans get off my property!"

The boys both turned on hearing her voice. They looked directly at her and didn't seem to notice me. They both smiled mockingly.

Harriet Edwards froze for a moment in fear. Then, as tears started leaking from her eyes, she croaked, "Just... leave."

"I told you before to shut up, you old bag," the taller one sneered. "Don't make me come up there and slap you."

Enraged, I charged up to the mouthy punk and grabbed him by the front of his jacket and lifted him right off the ground. As his feet dangled, I pulled him closer to my face so we were eye to eye.

"Do you see that woman over there on the porch?" I growled. "If you ever speak to her like that again, you better have somebody else with you. You know why?"

I paused for a second. When the sleaze ball didn't say anything, I answered my own question and said, "To pick you up after I knock you on your ass!"

Then, I flung him backwards and he landed flat on his back. He looked at up me hesitantly, but didn't say or do anything.

Out of the corner of my eye, I saw his companion start running at me. I pivoted to my left to face him. He brought his right fist back to throw a big old-fashioned haymaker. I never gave him the chance. As soon as his hand went back, I jumped forward and used my left forearm to block his punch while at the same time striking his chin with the heel of my right hand. As he started to reel backwards, I brought my right leg up and swept his legs out from under him. As he came down, I followed him and used my arms to drive him down to the ground.

When he landed, the air came out of his lungs with a sound like "oompf". I immediately turned to make sure the taller guy didn't have any ideas of attacking me. He wasn't there. I looked around and spotted him running toward the shed. Since I was sure the guy on the ground was unconscious and wasn't getting up anytime soon, I chased after the fleeing man.

He got to the old barn first and pounded on the door. I heard him scream, "Moose! Help me!"

As I reached the shed a second or two later, the door opened and a young man walked out of the barn. He was a little over six feet tall with brown, greasy hair. He was at least three hundred pounds with a huge potbelly. He wore no coat, choosing instead to wear only black sweat pants and an old, black, *Megadeth* T-shirt.

I recognized him from court. His name was Danny "Moose" Whitfield. My friend, Sandy Collins, had defended him several times for assault, bar fights, and the occasional larceny. He was well known in town as a bully, drunk, and all-around dirtbag.

Without a word, he raised his right hand. Expecting a punch, I got ready to block it. Instead, he pointed a .38 revolver at me.

"Get your hands up, motherfucker," he ordered.

I did as he asked.

Without looking away from me, Moose started talking to his friend.

"What's this piece of shit want, Kevin?" he grunted.

Kevin, suddenly brave now that his big buddy was pointing a gun at me, walked toward me with a cocky smile on his face.

"I don't know, man," he groaned. He pointed back to where his cohort lay on the ground. "He threw me to the ground and fucked up Jeff with some kung fu shit."

"Oh yeah," Moose replied, "and why did he do that?"

"I don't know, man." Kevin whined. "He was all pissed off cuz we told that old bitch to shut the fuck up."

Moose laughed. "She your momma or something?" he asked stupidly.

I said nothing. I had not considered that one of the people bothering Mrs. Edwards might be armed. I had expected a possible fight, but not this. I kept my eyes focused on his gun, hoping either for an opening to take it away from him or that he was too dumb to use it.

"Nothing to say, motherfucker?" he asked again.

He walked closer to me, holding the gun at his right side

"Who are you, man?" he demanded. When I said nothing, he screamed, "Who the fuck are you?"

I wanted to make a witty insult like they do in the movies. *James Bond* would have known the right thing to say. I just kept quiet and tried to focus my concentration on the revolver.

I was pretty sure Moose would eventually shoot me, either

because he lost his temper or to save face in front of his friends. That meant I was going to have to take the gun away from him first.

Over the years, Mr. Ito had demonstrated how to disarm an attacker with a gun. We worked on them in class and I had become quite proficient. However, I had never needed to actually use it in real life. In the dojo, we always used a fake wooden gun and there was no chance of getting shot and killed. What was pointed at me right now was solid steel and very real.

Moose just stared at me when I didn't answer. Before he could say or do anything else, Kevin yelled out, "Waste him, Moose!"

Moose shook his head. "Not yet, man. I want to make sure he ain't a cop. I ain't shooting no cop."

Moose glared at me intently. "So, you a cop, shithead?"

I realized that I had just found an opening. I was excited at the opportunity, but frightened as well. I knew that in a matter of seconds, I was going to attempt perhaps the most dangerous action of my life. If I did the technique incorrectly, I would almost certainly end up with a bullet in my gut.

"Yes," I finally said, "I'm a cop."

"Oh, bullshit," Kevin yelled in reply. "He's lying, Moose. Just shoot the fucker."

Moose was not so sure. He looked at me suspiciously, not knowing whether to believe me. After a few seconds, he said, "Prove it."

"I've got my badge on me," I said. "It's in my right rear pocket. I'll just get it and—"

"No fucking way," Moose interrupted. "You keep your hands up. I'll get your fucking badge."

Keeping the gun pointed at me, but at his right side, he reached out with his left hand toward my right hip. As he did, he looked away from me for the first time.

I grabbed the barrel of the gun with my right hand and pushed it hard to the left. I added my left hand to the gun and violently yanked it back down and to the right. Moose screamed as his trigger finger shattered and the gun came lose. He barely had time to react before I struck him in the face as hard as I could with the butt of the gun.

He fell backwards and landed flat on his butt. His lip was bleeding freely, but he barely noticed it. Instead, he was holding his right hand and screaming in agony. His right index finger was broken badly. Part of the bone was sticking right through the flesh and the finger was barely connected to his hand by a small strip of tissue. He was bleeding profusely.

"Oh shit," Kevin screamed in shock.

I whirled toward him. He was standing completely still, petrified in fear.

"Get down on the ground," I ordered.

Kevin didn't move. I moved the gun to my left hand and grabbed him with my right. I flung him down toward the ground. He landed on his left side.

"Get down," I yelled.

Kevin immediately turned to his stomach and put his hands on his head. He evidently had been arrested before. He knew the drill.

I pivoted so I could see Mrs. Edwards on the porch. As I did, I noticed that the first punk was still lying flat on the ground. Mrs. Edwards had a look of horror on her face.

"Mrs. Edwards!" I shouted, "please call 911 and tell them we need the police and an ambulance."

She waved her arm to signal she understood, before turning back into her house.

I put the gun into the back waistband of my jeans. I pulled off my jacket and my shirt. Then I put the jacket back on and zipped it.

I took my shirt and went over to Moose who was still screaming on the ground. I ripped a strip off of the shirt and used it to bind his bleeding finger as best I could. I told Moose to put pressure on it and not let go. It would only be a matter of minutes before the strips were completely soaked through with blood, but it would have to do.

I could hear multiple sirens now. They were getting closer and would arrive soon. Once they arrived, I knew I wouldn't be able to talk to these guys again. I decided I better speak now.

"Gentlemen," I said calmly, "I assume this is the last time I see you on this property?"

They both nodded vigorously.

CHAPTER TWELVE

I spent most of the evening at the Rockfield Police Station. The officers who arrived at the scene asked me to drive to the station to give my statement. I agreed.

When I got there, I was escorted to one of their interrogation rooms. I was told that one of the detectives would be there shortly. I took notice that the door was locked from the outside when the officer left.

As I waited, I looked around the room. There wasn't much to see. There was a large mirror on the far wall, which I knew was double-sided, so detectives could observe suspects being questioned. I had no idea if anyone was currently on the other side. Just in case, I smiled and waved at the mirror.

The walls were almost bare, but suitably dirty. In fact, the only thing on the walls besides dirt was an old clock that ticked loudly. There was one light I could see in the entire room. The only furniture was a metal table directly in front of the chair I was sitting on, as well as a much more comfortable looking chair on the other side of the table. Unlike my chair, that one had arms and a cushion on the seat. I guess the police wanted to be comfortable when they grilled their suspects.

I quickly stood and switched the chairs. If they were going to make me wait, I was using the comfy chair.

About ten minutes later, the lock clicked and the door opened. Rockfield Chief of Detectives Adam Richards entered. I groaned inwardly to myself. Richards and I had never warmed to one another. I always thought Richards was an arrogant, bellowing bully with delusions of grandeur. I could usually stand him for about thirty seconds. On a good day, I might last a minute. I was pretty sure it was not going to be a good day.

Although we were about the same height, that was the only physical resemblance. Richards was well over three hundred pounds, a substantial portion of which was in his belly. His poor gun belt strained to hold up the girth that sagged over it. He had an obvious drinker's nose and his hair was thin and unkempt. I could smell the booze the moment he entered the room. I wondered if I smelled it on his breath or if it was leaking out of his pores.

He walked over and sat on the metal chair that was intended for me. He realized that the chairs had been switched only after his bulbous behind landed, but he tried to hide his displeasure. He did not plan to give me the satisfaction of knowing it bothered him. Yet his eyes gave it all away. In my mind, I snickered.

Richards threw a thin case folder on the table in front of me.

"Care to guess what's in there, hot shot?" he asked arrogantly.

I was growing annoyed. After having a gun pointed at me, I was in no mood to deal with Adam Richards and his bullshit.

"Well," I said, trying to look thoughtful, "it's too small for your bottle of Jack Daniels."

"Cut the shit, Phelan," he growled. "There are statements in there from all three boys you assaulted."

I smiled. "Let me guess," I said. "They all claim that they

were minding their own business and I just showed up and viciously beat them up."

"That a confession?" Richards asked stupidly.

By this point, my patience was gone. I knew that even if Moose and his pals had pointed the finger at me, it would never withstand legal scrutiny. That being said, if Richards charged me, District Attorney Worthington would no doubt press the matter. Though I would eventually prevail, they would both make my life miserable for months.

"Maybe you should use your head, detective," I said. "First, Moose Whitfield is twenty-two years old. That makes him an adult. Second, do you really think Harriet Edwards invited those three upstanding citizens on her property?"

Richards just stared at me and said nothing. The only sound in the room was the ticking of the clock. It seemed much louder as the silence lengthened. I decided to press the issue.

"Look, Whitfield pulled a gun on me and—"

"You were the one found possessing the gun," Richards interrupted. "That's a felony, pal."

"I took the gun away from Moose after he threatened to shoot me," I continued, making a concerted effort not to lose my temper.

"That's not what Whitfield says," Richards shouted. "He says you pistol whipped him and his friends."

I laughed openly. "You know as well as I do that Moose Whitfield has been arrested multiple times for brawls. He lies as much as he drinks, which is considerable."

Richards opened his mouth, but I spoke before he could. It was clear he could not be reasoned with. I needed to try something else.

"I'm surprised you haven't seen him out and about," I said sarcastically. "Don't you guys see each other at the bars? Or do you just drink alone?"

Richards slammed his fists on the table and stood up menacingly. I stood as well. My goal was to get him angry, but I had no intention of attacking the big slob. I just wanted to be ready if he decided to throw a punch.

We just looked at each other for a few seconds before the door opened again and a calm but authoritative voice announced, "Both of you sit down, now."

I recognized the voice immediately. It belonged to Chief Jim Taylor.

Jim Taylor was hard-nosed and no nonsense. Both respected and feared by his men, he had served as Police Chief for a little over thirty years. As always, he had his brown, wooden, billiard pipe in his mouth. His aromatic tobacco smoke offered an alternative to Richards' whiskey and sweat smell.

Richards turned toward Taylor and stood at attention. I wasn't about to stand at attention, but had no problem showing respect to the chief. I already owed him a big favor because he had helped Dom and me out of a particularly sticky situation a few months earlier. During a confrontation Dom and I had with Worthington, Dom punched him and broke his nose. We were facing potential criminal charges. Taylor somehow made the charges disappear. Neither of us knew how he accomplished it, but we both knew he would one day call in that favor.

On top of that, Jim Taylor was the kind of guy whose presence alone commanded attention and respect.

Once it was clear that order had been restored, Taylor addressed Richards first.

"Detective, I'll take over from here," he said softly.

Richards glared angrily at me. He looked ready to chew nails and spit them at me. Instead, he simply replied, "Yes, sir," and left the room.

As soon as the door closed behind Richards, Chief Taylor took a long draw on his pipe. He held the smoke in his mouth for a few seconds before slowly releasing it out of his mouth. Then, he sat in the chair previously occupied by Richards and extended his hand palm up toward my chair. I sat down.

"You were watching behind the mirror?" I asked.

Taylor nodded. He then opened the file Richards had left on the table and started reading. As he did, he chuckled.

"Damn jackass," he mumbled.

When he finished reading, he closed the file and sat back in the chair.

"You needn't worry," he announced. "No charges are being filed against you."

"Good," I answered. "Richards sure made it seem like he planned to hold me."

"I don't know if he was fucking with you or if his brain is completely marinated in hooch," he replied.

He took another draw on his pipe before continuing.

"I already spoke to Harriet Edwards. She confirms that you were there to help her deal with those mutts," he said.

"Hooligans, you mean," I offered.

"Yeah, hoodlums and hooligans." Taylor said, starting to laugh. "She's quite the lady."

"So, where do we go from here?" I asked. "Am I free to go?"

"Yeah, you can leave whenever you want," the chief responded. "Whitfield is being charged with misdemeanor possession of a weapon. Turns out the gun he pulled on you was registered to his daddy."

He took the pipe out of his mouth and held it in his left hand.

"I could have charged him with a felony," he continued, "but I figure having his finger nearly fucking ripped off and one of his teeth knocked out should count for some of the punishment."

"Chief, with all due respect," I said, "this guy pointed a gun at me and was going to shoot me."

"Don't worry, Connor," Taylor replied, "he'll do several months in county jail and I'll make sure my men keep a close eye on him when he gets out. He won't bother you again. Trust me."

I didn't bother arguing. The last time Jim Taylor had asked me to trust him, everything worked out exactly as he predicted. I knew his word was good.

"What about the other two?" I asked.

"I wasn't going to charge them with anything," Taylor answered. "Neither one has a record. Besides, one has a broken rib and though the other isn't hurt, he's scared shitless."

We both laughed.

"You said you weren't going to charge them," I pressed. "Something change your mind?"

"Yeah, Harriet Edwards," Taylor said. "When I told her, she got all bent out of shape. She absolutely insisted that all three 'hoodlums' be charged with trespassing."

"And you gave in?" I asked.

"She was my second-grade teacher too," Taylor said, smiling widely. "So, I gave them appearance tickets in city court. I sent one of them home and had the other taken to the emergency room."

When Taylor didn't say anything else for nearly thirty seconds, I stood to leave.

"You mind staying for a minute, Connor?" the chief asked.

I quickly resumed my seat.

"Sure, what's on your mind?" I asked.

Taylor put his pipe back in his mouth and took a long drag on it. As he released the smoke, he seemed to be considering his words carefully.

"How's John Hardy's case coming along?" he finally asked.

It was very unusual for the chief of police to ask an attorney about his defense for someone charged with murder. I had to play along. I figured Taylor either had something he wanted to tell me or something about the case was bothering him.

"To be straight with you, chief, the whole case is crap, except for the DNA evidence," I said. "That has me concerned."

"You think Hardy did it?" Taylor asked.

If I was being honest with myself, I was having serious doubts. Hardy's hair and DNA were found on the victim's clothes. That alone was enough for a jury to convict him. They would deliberate for no more than fifteen minutes. DNA was the modern smoking gun.

Yet, the Judge John Hardy I knew and respected would never have even considered such a thing. He was a man who dedicated his life to justice. His entire career had been spent as a prosecutor and as a judge.

A few months ago, he assigned me to be special prosecutor on a murder case where he knew the person being charged was innocent. He did it because he knew I needed a wake-up call, and because he was confident I would unmask the real murderer in short order.

Taylor saw the hesitation in my eyes. He took the pipe out of his mouth, leaned forward, and pointed his finger at me.

"I've known John Hardy as long as I can remember," he said sternly. "There is no way on God's green Earth that he murdered anybody."

"How do you explain the hair and the DNA?" I said challengingly.

"I don't," Taylor said immediately. "I just know John Hardy, and John Hardy is no murderer."

His tone was direct and straight to the point. In my heart, I knew he was right. I felt almost ashamed that I had even considered Hardy might be guilty. The DNA was damning, but

John Hardy was not a murderer. There must be an explanation for his hair being at the scene. I just had to find it.

The theory of the prosecution was that Hardy's hair got there because he murdered Gilbert Russell in cold blood. Ever since I learned of the hair evidence, I had been racking my brain trying to think of an innocent explanation. No matter how hard I tried, I simply could not come up with anything even remotely reasonable.

After reading the police file Dom had gotten for me, something else had been gnawing at me. Reports about the hair had been removed from the file. Why? The lab report was still there. Anyone reading the file would know about the evidence. My mind starting racing. What did removing those reports prevent me from knowing? I realized I had an opportunity here to possibly get some answers.

"Who found the hair?" I asked.

Taylor's face was like stone. "That's the million-dollar question," he said.

"Well, who was it?" I demanded.

"I don't know," Taylor replied.

"How could you not know?" I pressed. "If those reports were in the file and then removed, someone had to—"

"I don't know who found it," Taylor repeated, a little more loudly. "None of my detectives did, and whatever reports existed were taken by Worthington's office and never actually made it into our file."

"Are you saying the state police lab made it up?" I asked almost incredulously.

"No," Taylor answered, shaking his head vigorously. "I called the head of the lab. Hairs were brought to them and they did test them. The test is legit."

"But who gave them the hair?" I asked.

"You're not going to like it," Taylor answered.

"Wait a minute," I replied, "you said you weren't sure who found the hair. Do you know who it was or not?"

"I don't know if he initially found the evidence," Taylor continued, "but I know he brought it to the lab."

I was beyond tired of this shell game. "Who are you talking about?" I demanded.

Taylor looked me squarely in the eyes. When he spoke again, I felt a cold shiver run down my spine and through my arms.

"It was Roger Billingsley."

CHAPTER THIRTEEN

I did not sleep well that night. I kept hearing the voice of Jim Taylor over and over again. *Roger Billingsley.* Roger Billingsley had brought the hair to the police lab.

For a moment at the police station, I had the solution. Hardy was innocent. The hair had been planted and Hardy framed for murder. The thought had raced through me like electricity, almost making my fingers tingle with excitement. But that feeling was gone in an instant.

Worse, if what Jim Taylor told me was true, then Bills had done something I would never have believed possible. He had lied to me. He said he was not on the case because Worthington felt he was too close to Hardy. Yet, according to Jim Taylor, another man known for his honesty, Bills was the one who brought the hair to the lab for testing.

My emotions went back and forth. First, I felt absolute anger at Billingsley's betrayal. "If I see something that ain't kosher, I'll contact you," he had said. How could he have lied in such a despicable way?

Then, I felt a stunning numbness as I considered that the evidence before me showed John Hardy to be a murderer and

Roger Billingsley to be a liar. These were both men I looked up to and considered mentors. To have both of them fall from grace in such a manner was almost too shocking to bear. I desperately tried to put this out of my mind. There had to be a logical answer to all of this. If only I could find it.

That night, I tossed and turned in my bed for hours. trying to reconcile the concepts of Hardy being innocent and Billingsley being the one who found the hair and incriminating DNA. They were pieces of the puzzle that didn't seem to fit. Eventually I fell asleep, but without an answer to my vexing riddle.

The next morning, I went straight to my office. I didn't bother stopping for breakfast. I wasn't hungry. I barely heard Casey speaking as I walked past her. I slumped into my chair and tossed the case file onto the desk. Worthington was winning the game. Even my morning coffee offered little solace.

I was still lost in deep and disturbing thought when I was snapped back to reality by the realization that someone was sitting in one of my client chairs. It was Casey. She seemed genuinely concerned.

"Connor, are you okay?" she asked. "You seem completely lost. I buzzed you twice. I came in here to make sure you hadn't fallen asleep."

I tried to smile reassuringly, but found it nearly impossible. So much of what I believed in had crumbled in just a few days.

"No, I'm not," I finally admitted.

"Tell me about it," she offered.

So, I did. I related the events at Harriet Edwards' home the night before, the confrontation with Detective Richards, and the devastating revelation from Jim Taylor. She said nothing as I spoke, though she grinned while I described taking the gun away from Moose Whitfield.

When I finished, she thought for a moment. Then, she stood

and walked toward the door. She stopped in the doorway and turned back.

"Don't give up, Connor," she said. "You always find a way to deal with the toughest cases."

I raised my hand to protest, but she waved me off.

"Remember when I first started working here?" she asked. "I was a disaster for the first week or two. I couldn't seem to do anything right."

I did remember. It had only been the first few days, not two weeks. Casey had been very nervous and made several pretty significant mistakes, including losing a trial memorandum that was due that very day. We spent nearly an hour tearing the office apart before she embarrassingly realized it was in her car.

'You remember what you told me?" Casey asked.

"Yes," I answered. "I told you that you had the talent to do this job. All you had to do was relax and trust yourself."

"You were right," she added. "And look at how wonderful I am now."

I smiled and nodded my head in acknowledgement.

"Take your own advice, Connor," continued Casey in a reassuring voice. "You're the best. You'll figure it out. You always do."

I was still considering her words as she closed the door behind her.

The police file Dom had given me was lying on my desk. I opened it and started reading it yet again. Maybe I could find the answer there. I had not even finished the first page when my intercom buzzed. I pressed the button without saying a word.

"Speaking of wonderful," Casey's voice boomed out, no longer reassuring, but back to its normal acerbic tone, "guess who's here?"

"Send Dom in," I answered.

A few seconds later, my door opened and Dom came in. As

always, he was dressed in jeans, a button-down shirt, and his cowboy hat and boots. The color of his clothes changed daily, but never the style. He also never ceased to have his Colt .45 on his hip. At least I could always depend on that.

He started to take a seat, but I stood up suddenly, startling him slightly.

"Let's go, boss," I announced. "You're driving."

"Sure, but where are we going?" Dom answered.

"You and I are going to see Judge Hardy," I said. "I have to talk to him about the latest development."

"Huh," Dom said, clearly confused.

"I'll tell you on the way," I said, as I walked out the door.

As Dom and I were leaving, Casey was on the phone and it was clear that the person on the other line was giving her a very hard time.

"Please hold," she announced firmly, before slamming her index finger down hard on the red hold button.

"Connor," she called to me, "Old Iron Girdle is on the phone demanding an update on Hardy's case. She's driving me crazy because she won't take no for an answer."

"She's going to have to, because I haven't got time to talk to her right now," I replied. "Just tell her I'll get back to her when I can."

Casey shot me a look of annoyance, but quickly recovered.

"Where are you going?" she asked.

"I'm off to relax and trust myself," I answered with a wink.

"About time," Casey said sarcastically.

When we reached Dom's truck, I told him to drive to Judge Hardy's home. On the way, I told him all about the previous evening's events and the conversation I had with Jim Taylor. When I finished, Dom seemed stunned.

"Holy shit," he finally breathed. "So, what's next?"

"I have to talk to Hardy," I said. "I want to hear his response to all of this."

A few minutes later, we arrived at Hardy's house. The judge lived in a large colonial style home. It was white with black shutters on all of the nine windows on the front. The house and the windows were completely symmetric; a collection of squares and rectangles. The front door was at the top of a stone staircase and surrounded by a porch held up by four columns, two on either side. It was plain in design, but grandiose in appearance.

Hardy answered on my second knock. He seemed very pleased to see us.

"Connor, my boy," he announced jovially, "please come in." When he saw Dom, Hardy immediately extended his hand. "Good to see you, Investigator Bryce."

"Hello, Your Honor," Bryce said respectfully, as he shook the judge's hand.

"Well don't just stand there," Hardy shouted enthusiastically. "Come on in."

He led us to the right of the huge staircase in the middle of the hall and into his parlor. It was magnificent. Against the center wall was a fireplace with an ornate antique mirror above it. A huge crystal chandelier hung from the ceiling. On the walls were very old portraits, which I presumed were Hardy's ancestors. On the far side of the room was a grand piano. Its highly polished black wood gleamed in the sunlight that shone through the luxurious curtains on the window behind it.

John took a seat in a large antique chair and pointed to a couch that was equally old and matched the chair.

"Sit, gentlemen," he bellowed. "Be comfortable."

We had no sooner sat down when Hardy started talking again.

"I can tell by the look on your face, Connor, that this is not a social call," he said in a more serious tone. "Is there bad news?"

I inhaled sharply before speaking. "John, they have your DNA at the scene of the crime."

Hardy's eyes widened in surprise. "That's not possible," he insisted.

"It is possible," I insisted. "They found four of your hairs on Russell's body and they got DNA from one of them. It matched yours."

"That can't be," Hardy responded, his face showing shock and growing concern.

"It is," I pressed, "and I need to know how it got there."

Hardy seemed befuddled. "I have no idea," he croaked. "I never had any physical contact with that loathsome creature. I only saw him in court and he was never within ten feet of me."

"Then how did the hair get on his clothes?" I demanded.

"I don't know," Hardy shouted, pounding his fist on the arm of his chair. "It must have been planted by someone."

I shook my head. This seemed to infuriate Hardy.

"What do you mean, no?" he screamed. "I didn't kill that man! If my DNA is there, then somebody put it there."

"John," I said in a voice I was desperately trying to make sound calm, "They were found and brought to the lab by Roger Billingsley."

There was genuine fear on Hardy's face now. "Bills?" he said, almost in stunned disbelief.

After a moment of silence, Hardy regained his composure. When he spoke again, his voice was strong and solid.

"Connor, there are two things you can take to the bank," Hardy announced, as if giving a campaign speech. "First, Roger Billingsley doesn't lie. Second, I did not kill Gilbert Russell."

I looked directly into Hardy's eyes as he spoke. I saw no

hesitation, no glimmer of deception. He was either telling the truth or he was the best damn liar I had ever seen.

Inside of me, the battle between my heart and my head raged. All of the evidence pointed directly at Hardy. I had not found anything that pointed at anyone else. Yet, in my heart and in my gut, I was certain that Hardy was telling the truth and had not killed Russell.

Of course, I had also been certain that Bills would never lie to me. I decided not to share that with Hardy. I had no desire to discuss it, debate it, or even talk about it. Besides, if I did announce Billingsley's lie, Hardy could have just used that to justify his claim of innocence.

"How can both of those things be true?" I said accusingly.

"Bills may have found the hair," Hardy said forcefully, "but somebody else put it there."

Nobody said anything for a while and the room was deathly quiet.

"Your Honor," Dom said, breaking the tense silence. "Let's assume for a minute that someone planted the evidence against you. Who would want to frame you?"

"Well," Hardy replied, "when you've put as many people in prison as I have, you make a lot of enemies. Any one of those criminals would want me taken down."

I shook my head. "No, they might have the motive," I said, "but they wouldn't have the means."

"Why not?" Hardy asked.

"Think about it, John," I pressed. "How would any of those defendants have been able to get some of your hair without you knowing it? You been attacked by anybody recently?"

"Can't say that I have, my boy," Hardy said, his jovial personality beginning to reassert itself. "Then again, at my age, my hair just falls out on its own."

Hardy and Dom laughed. I did not.

"Are we to believe that some of these defendants have been following you around and collecting your hair as it falls out of your scalp?" I asked. "How do you think a jury would react to that argument?"

The smile left Hardy and Dom's faces instantly.

"They would find me guilty," Hardy admitted sadly.

"Precisely," I said.

Hardy stood up. There was a hint of panic in his eyes.

"Connor, I swear to you, I did not kill that son of a bitch!" Hardy yelled. "If they found my hair on that guy, then somebody planted it there!"

I said nothing. Part of me believed him, but lingering doubt nipped at my heels.

When I did not reply, Hardy spoke again.

"Don't give up on me, Connor," Hardy pleaded. "I need you to find out who killed Russell and who is trying to frame me."

I stood as well. "I will try, John," I said softly.

Hardy walked up to me and put his hands on my shoulders.

"I have never lied to you Connor," he said solemnly. "Keep searching for the truth. You're my only hope, son."

I also believed Bills would never lie to me either, I thought. Regardless, I was determined to learn the truth one way or the other. I would find out who was lying and who was telling the truth. I would also discover who murdered Gilbert Russell. I just hoped it wouldn't be John Hardy.

CHAPTER FOURTEEN

om and I left Hardy's opulent home and went right to his truck. We were several blocks away before either of us spoke.

"So, where are we heading?" Dom asked. "Back to the office?"

I shook my head. I knew Hardy's only chance was to prove that someone had planted the incriminating evidence. I had no idea who had done that, and frankly had serious doubts if someone really had done so. Nevertheless, with no real defense and no leads, our only option was to start at the beginning.

"Let's go talk to Al and Jamie Lawson," I said.

Dom turned his truck around without comment. We arrived at the Lawsons' home about fifteen minutes later.

This home was quite different than Hardy's lavish estate. The Lawsons lived in a small, faded yellow farmhouse. There was a large brick chimney on the left side of the house, rising from the ground and reaching several feet above the top of the roof. The front porch ran the entire width of the house and was held up with columns. Unlike Hardy's stone porch columns, these were made of wood. Once, they had been beautiful, but time and weather had caused the paint to peel away giving it a dilapidated look.

Hardy's porch was at the top of a grand stone staircase. The Lawsons' porch was directly on the ground. One only had to step up about six inches to reach the door.

Jamie Lawson was sitting on an old rocking chair on the porch as we approached. She was about thirty with short blonde hair. Her eyes had a look of tired sadness that dominated her entire face.

She made an effort to smile and be friendly, but it was apparent that grief and sorrow still held a firm grip on her entire being.

"May I help you?" she asked, almost without emotion.

"Ma'am, my name is Connor Phelan," I began, "and this is Dom Bryce, my investigator."

She extended her hand politely, but did not get out of the chair. Dom and I both shook her hand.

"I'm defending John Hardy against charges of murder," I explained. "May we speak for a few minutes?"

When Jamie heard the name John Hardy, there was the first glimmer of emotion in her eyes. The look was one of hatred and anger. It was only there for just a moment.

She looked around and pointed to a second rocking chair on the porch. "Please, have a seat," she said.

I sat, but there was not a third chair for Dom. He just shrugged and leaned against one of the old wooden columns holding up the porch. As big as he was, I hoped he wouldn't bring the whole damn thing down on us.

"Mrs. Lawson," I said, "I'm sorry to have to bring all of this up, but I'm trying to find out who murdered Gilbert Russell."

"That was no murder," she said abruptly. "That was the execution that monster deserved for killing my..."

The words caught in her throat as she tried to stifle the emotion and tears threatening to burst out of her.

"Pardon me, Mr. Phelan, but I..."

"No need to apologize, ma'am," I said quickly.

She held up her hand to stop me. "No," she said, "I'm a good Christian woman. I'm not supposed to take pleasure in another's death. But, God forgive me, I'm glad that unimaginable bastard is dead. He —"

"I understand," I interrupted. "Gilbert Russell was a despicable human being. My job is to prove that John Hardy wasn't the one who killed him. To do that, I have to figure out who did."

The anger returned to Jamie's eyes. "And you think that I or my husband did it?"

"You have to admit," I said calmly, "you and your husband both wanted him dead."

"You're damn right, we did," she shouted, tears streaming down her cheeks. "He had it coming and we're both glad he's dead."

I started to speak, but she pointed her finger at me, so I waited.

"Neither of us killed him," she said sternly.

I took a breath before continuing. "I'm sure the police asked you this already, ma'am, but where were you and your husband the night Gilbert Russell died?"

"Right here," she said immediately, a mixture of anger and frustration covering her face. "Al and I were in our bed sleeping that night. And before you even ask, no, there wasn't anybody else here."

I held up my hands with my palms facing her almost as a sign of surrender.

"Ma'am, I appreciate you taking the time to speak with me," I said. "Is your husband around today?"

She shook her head and wiped away her tears with her thumbs.

"He's over at his mother's horse farm," she said. "It's about two miles up this same road. He goes there nearly every day to care for the place. Been doing so ever since she passed away."

I thanked Mrs. Lawson for her time and offered her my condolences. She accepted both politely, though I knew from experience that she was likely sick to death of all the condolences and well wishes.

I thought back to when Melissa and I had got married and we'd had our entire life mapped out in almost every detail. After her death, I'd been alone and living day to day without even any idea what I would order for lunch, let alone what I would do for the rest of my life. In the months that followed, everyone had offered me their condolences: "If there is anything I can do for you, let me know," they had all said. I knew they meant well, just as I just had. But I was eventually so fed up with hearing it that the words almost made me angry. Now, here I was doing the same thing. How ironic, I thought.

Dom and I made our way back to his truck. Neither of us had to say anything. We both knew we were heading right to Agnes Lawson's horse farm.

As Jamie Lawson had said, the farm was almost exactly two miles down the road. The two large pastures for the horses were surrounded by split-wood paddock fencing. Each section of the fence had four cross beams. It was painted white where it faced the road. However, the fence on the inside of the driveway was not painted at all.

Five or six horses grazed lazily from within the fence. They didn't seem to care or notice when Dom pulled his truck onto the long driveway. Dom drove in a couple hundred feet and stopped by a very large horse barn. It had once been white, though the roof was newer and its dark shingles gave a nice contrast to the dingy white walls.

The driveway forked at this point. One direction turned sharply left and ran along the front of the barn. The other moved slightly to the right and went past the barn toward a gray farmhouse some distance away.

Dom looked over to me. "Which way, boss?" he asked.

I looked around. To our left, I saw Al Lawson. He was near the huge front entrance to the barn where the horses were walked out to the pasture. He was wearing a brown jacket and a straw hat.

"Pull over to the side of the barn and park," I said. "We can walk from here."

Dom drove almost to the end of the side of the barn and parked. We walked to where Al Lawson stood. He was moving bales of hay. We got to the fence itself and then waved to him.

When Lawson saw us, he walked over to his side of the fence.

"What can I do for you, boys?" he asked.

"Mr. Lawson, I'm Connor Phelan and this—"

"I know who you are, Connor," he barked. "Hell, I've known Dom here for more years that I want to count."

Dom extended his hand and they shook.

"How you doing, Al?" he asked.

"Not too bad, all things he considered," he replied. "Just trying to keep Momma's horse farm going. Been in the family for over a hundred years."

"I know," Dom said. "I remember your daddy riding them horses and shoveling manure."

Lawson laughed slightly. "Yeah," he said, seeming to reminisce, "Daddy could shovel shit with the best of them."

We all laughed, but Lawson quickly got to the point. "I

highly doubt you guys are here to talk about my daddy," he said. "What's on your mind?"

Dom looked at me, but I nodded my approval that he should do the talking.

"Al, I think you know that Connor here is representing Judge Hardy," Dom said.

"I do," Lawson said.

"Well, if Hardy didn't kill that rat bastard," Dom said in his eloquent way, "we need to find out who did."

Lawson nodded his head. "So, I reckon you need to ask me if I killed the son of a bitch."

"That's about right," Dom said.

"Dom, I wish I had. I truly do," Lawson said. "But, so help me, I didn't. I was home that night with my wife."

I decided to say something.

"Mr. Lawson, I hope you know that we take no pleasure in asking you about this, but we have—"

"That's all right, son," he said quickly. "I threatened him just like the judge did. Only natural that people would think I killed him. Hell, I think the only one who wanted him dead more than me and my wife was Momma. She just loved my little Jillie. Broke her heart when they found her."

He looked away when his tears began to fall. Dom and I waited for a moment while he regained his composure. When he turned back, I resumed our discussion.

"Your mother and Jill were close?" I asked.

"They were two peas in a pod," he replied, a slight smile returning to his lips. "Momma thought the sun rose and set on my baby girl."

Then, he got an odd look on his face, as he seemed to consider my question.

"Wait a minute," he said, showing just a hint of annoyance.

"My momma died a few weeks before they found that scum hanging from a tree. She couldn't have killed him."

"I wasn't suggesting that," I responded. "I know she passed a few weeks ago."

"Russell killed her too," Lawson said suddenly.

"What?" I said, caught by surprise at his remark. "I was under the impression that Aggie Lawson died of natural causes."

"Doctors say it was a heart attack," Lawson replied coldly. "But I know better. Momma died of a broken heart. When they told us they had found Jillie's body, it just took the life out of her. Damn near killed me too."

I understood Lawson's grief and his anger. I had been through both after my wife and son died. I knew from experience that further questioning wasn't going to get us very much. Both Al Lawson and his wife had motive, but neither was going to admit guilt.

"Look, Mr. Lawson," I said, "I'm sure that—"

No, you look," Lawson said sharply, "I don't know who killed Gilbert Russell. But, if you find out, let me know. I want to shake the guy's hand."

Without another word, Dom and I turned and walked to his truck. As we did, thoughts rushed through my mind like a tornado. The emotions of this case and my own doubts concerning John Hardy were nearly impossible to keep controlled. I felt that both of the Lawsons had been believable in their answers. They both hated Russell and with good reason. Both openly admitted their desire to have been the one who killed their daughter's murderer. But, both denied to their displeasure that they had not killed him. I believed them, and that did not help John Hardy.

"Hey, Connor," I heard Dom shout. "Where the fuck are you going?"

I looked back and realized that in my inward reflection, I

had walked nearly fifty feet past the truck. I was actually beyond the barn.

"Sorry, boss," I yelled out, slightly embarrassed, and started walking back to the truck. As I did, I looked to my right and my breath caught in my throat.

Parked behind the barn was a silver 1979 Ford Ranger pick-up. It was old, dirty, and very rusty. It looked exactly like the truck in the DVD.

"Dom, take a look at this," I said, before trotting over to the truck.

Dom came around the barn. When he saw the pickup, he had the same reaction as I did.

"Holy shit," he said. "Looks like the same fucking truck."

"Sure does," I said.

I took a look at the tires. There was some mud on them. It wasn't exactly fresh, but it wasn't very old either. The truck had been moved somewhat recently.

I pulled my cell phone out of my pocket and started taking pictures of the truck from every angle. I started with the tires and then worked my way completely around. I took extra photos of the front half of the passenger side. This was the side seen on the DVD and I wanted to compare it carefully.

When I got to the driver's side door, I noticed that the window was open. I leaned through the window to see inside.

"You like Momma's truck?"

The voice of Al Lawson startled me. I instinctively stood up and banged my head and neck on the top of the car window. I grunted in pain and then carefully backed out to avoid further damage.

Lawson didn't seem angry that I was looking in the truck, so I played along.

"She still run?" I asked.

"Should," Lawson replied, "I haven't started it since

Momma died, but she used it right up until a day or two before she died."

Aggie Lawson died weeks ago, I thought, but this truck had been moved since then. Maybe I had misjudged Al Lawson's sincerity when he denied being the killer.

"She drove it often?" Dom asked.

"No, not in the last few years," Lawson replied. "She used to take it to the market once in a while. But mostly over the last few years, she drove it twice a week. On Sundays, she went to church and on Wednesdays, she went to her ladies' club."

"Ladies club?" I asked.

"Well, that's what they called it," Lawson said. "She and some of her friends met every Wednesday and played Mahjong. They did that every week going back thirty years or more."

I looked at Dom. He just shrugged.

"If you want to start it up," Lawson continued, "Momma always kept the keys in the visor. Never locked the darn thing."

I leaned back into the car – carefully this time – and slid the visor down slightly. The keys were there. I opened the door and got in. I was not surprised that the truck started immediately. Odd for an engine that according to Al Lawson had not been turned over in several weeks.

I felt exhilarated. I finally had some evidence that I could use. I had my first real suspect.

CHAPTER FIFTEEN

A s Dom and I left Aggie Lawson's farm, our conversation focused on the old pick-up truck.

"Finally, we have something to work with," I said. "I still have to compare the pictures with the DVD, but I am certain they match."

"I don't think there's any doubt," Dom agreed. "It's the same truck. May not help us as much as you think though."

"What are you talking about?" I demanded. "We just found the truck used in the murder. That puts Al Lawson right at the top of the list of suspects."

"Maybe," Dom replied.

I couldn't understand why Dom wasn't as excited as I was. This was a major development in the case; perhaps our biggest break thus far. Still, Dom was a top-notch investigator. If he had reservations, he probably had a good reason.

"What's bugging you, boss?" I asked.

"Don't get me wrong, Connor, it's a big find," Dom said frowning, "but it's not the smoking gun you think it is."

"How do you figure?" I asked.

"The keys are there for anyone to use," he continued. "Plus, there's something else you don't know."

"What's that?" I demanded.

"In the last year or so of her life, Aggie Lawson was dating Judge Hardy," he said. "Worthington certainly knows that, and if we bring forth the truck without any more evidence—"

"He will claim that Hardy used the truck to commit the crime," I said, completing his sentence.

This case was like a roller coaster. We learn something that brings us up with excitement, only to find out something else that plunges us back down.

"Damn it," I shouted, pounding my fist down on my thigh. "I can see it now. Worthington will put Al Lawson on the stand to tell the jury how devastated his mother was. Then, that slimy worm will argue that Hardy did it for his sweetheart."

I let out a scream in frustration.

For the next few miles, neither of us said anything. Finally, I started talking, more to think out loud than have a conversation.

"Well, we know the truck was used in the murder," I said. "We know that both the Lawsons and Judge Hardy had access to the truck and could have used it since the keys were in the visor."

"And all three had motive," Dom added. "So, we got nothing."

"Aw, shit," I grunted.

Dom looked over at me. When he saw the look in my eyes, he changed his tone.

"I'll do a full background check on Al and Jamie Lawson tonight," he said. "Maybe I'll find something. Meanwhile, let's get an early lunch. There's a diner about a mile out with some great chili. The only thing hotter than that chili is this waitress there named Maxine. Connor, you should see her. She's got a set of legs on her that..."

I started tuning out as Dom further described Maxine. My mind wandered back to the Russell murder. In my career, I had handled many cases. None had been as frustrating as this one.

In truth, if I was prosecuting, this would be a really simple matter. The DNA of John Hardy was found on the victim's clothes. Case closed. However, from the defense perspective, or more precisely from John Hardy's perspective, the task was more Herculean.

Once again, as it had been nearly from the beginning, it all came back to the damn DNA. If his DNA was legitimately found on Gilbert Russell, then John Hardy was guilty and going to prison. To get Hardy exonerated, I had to prove either that the lab test was flawed or that somebody planted the evidence.

Demonstrating to a jury that the lab's test was defective would be nearly impossible. Juries love forensic evidence and rarely set it aside. Too many people watch *Forensic Files* and *CSI*. I'd have a better chance of sprouting feathers.

Proving that the hair was planted would be almost as difficult. Roger Billingsley was as solid as a rock on the witness stand. There were few better. Even if I could destroy his credibility, which I doubted, I would be saving one man I respected at the cost of another.

As I considered it further, I felt feelings of anger and betrayal return. How could Bills have lied to me? It seemed so out of character. But, if he had lied, then why was I even slightly concerned about ripping him apart on the witness stand? Didn't he deserve it?

"Connor? You in there?"

Dom's voice broke my concentration and brought me back from my troubled thoughts. I looked around and saw that we had arrived at our destination, Jim's Diner.

It was a run-down, metal building that looked like it might have been a railroad car fifty years ago. It was repainted blue and silver, and a red neon light in the window flashed, "open". It was not exactly the most appetizing sight.

"That's the second time this morning you've been lost in your own head," Dom scolded. "You, ok?"

"I'm fine," I lied. "I just can't believe Bills lied to me."

Dom grabbed me by the arm. "Let me tell you something right now," he barked angrily. "I've known Bills a hell of a lot longer than you, and that man doesn't lie."

"Does Jim Taylor lie?" I shouted back.

"Hell, no," Dom shouted right back.

"Well, one of them has," I insisted.

"Hardly likely," Dom said, but with a little less gusto.

I told him about Jim Taylor calling the lab and finding out that Bills had brought the hair sample in for testing. I also told him about my phone conversation with Bills where he said he was never on the case. When I finished, Dom considered what I had said for a few seconds before he responded.

"There's got to be more to the story that we just don't know," he said firmly. "Those men don't lie. You can count on that like death and taxes."

"Dom, I've thought about this every which way," I said. "If either one is telling the truth, then the other must be lying."

"No, way," Dom pressed.

I tried to argue my point, but Dom signaled me to stop.

"Let's go in and eat," he said more calmly. "While we do, give Bills a call. I know the guy. There's more going on here."

I nodded. "Fine," I said. "Let's eat."

The inside of the diner was much better than the outside, though it was a low bar by comparison. There were two or three tables, but the majority of the interior was taken up by a long counter that ran nearly the length of the room. Eleven round padded stools were bolted into the floor in front of it.

Behind the counter was a large metal grill with an immense

amount of grease. Multiple burgers were cooking while a heavyset man in an old apron stood over them with his spatula.

The other person behind the counter had to be Maxine. If the tight waitress outfit didn't give it away, her teased bleached blond hair à la 1985 did. She came over as Dom and I each took a stool.

"Dom Bryce, if you ain't a sight for sore eyes, sugar," she said in-between loud chomps of her gum.

Dom smiled so wide that I thought his face might break.

"Not looking as good as you, darling," he said, in a tone that I assume he thought was appealing.

"Who's your cute friend?" she said to Dom, eyeing me like a steak.

"This is my buddy, Connor Phelan," Dom announced, before turning to me. "Connor, this is Maxine. But, don't you get any ideas. She's my sugar momma."

I thought I might be sick, but I forced a polite smile.

"Nice to meet you," I said.

"What can I get you, honey?" Maxine said.

"Dom says the chili here is good," I answered.

"You bet your hiney, sweetie," she answered exuberantly. "Best around."

"I guess I'll try that," I said.

"Make it two," Dom announced. "And a couple of cold beers too."

"You got it, sugar," Maxine purred, as she wrote our order down.

A few minutes later, our food and beers arrived. I had to admit that Dom was right. The place didn't look like much, but the chili was fantastic.

When we finished our lunch, Dom ordered dessert. Shortly thereafter, Maxine brought a slice of pie that was buried in a mound of whipped cream.

"Here you go, sugar," Maxine said. "Just the way you like it."

Dom smiled and dug in. He stopped for just a second so he could look at Maxine's ass as she walked away. She obviously knew he was looking because she stopped, looked over her shoulder, and shimmied for just a second.

Dom hooted like a horny teenager. Maxine smiled and walked away. Dom took one more look at her posterior, and then dug into the pie like a man possessed.

"You going to have some pie with that whipped cream?" I asked.

"Don't knock it until you try it," he replied, without waiting to swallow his food.

I told Dom I was going to step outside to make a call. I left him to enjoy his quickly depleting dessert. Besides, one more verbal exchange between Dom and Maxine would have resulted in my chili coming back up.

I walked out of the diner and hopped into the passenger seat of the truck. I got my cell phone out of my jacket pocket and called Bills. He answered on the first ring.

"How you doing, boy?" he said, as if there was nothing wrong.

"Hey, Bills," I said, "can you talk freely right now?"

"Sure can," he replied, "I was going to call you shortly anyway."

I wanted to be patient on this call, but I needed to know why he lied to me. So, I forgot about patience and went right to the point.

"Why didn't you tell me that you were the one who brought the hair sample to the lab?" I challenged.

"What the hell are you talking about?" he answered. "I did no such thing."

"Jim Taylor says you brought the hair to the lab," I said,

barely keeping my voice under control. "You told me you had nothing to do whatsoever with Hardy's case."

"And I don't," Bills insisted.

"Jim Taylor doesn't lie," I pressed.

"And neither do I," Bills shouted back.

"Bills, both statements can't be true," I said.

"No, they can't," he admitted. "Look, I understand why you're upset. I know Chief Taylor very well. If he told you that, then he believes it, but I'm telling you that he's mistaken."

I wasn't sure what to think or say. I'd worked with Roger Billingsley both in the District Attorney's Office and as a private practice attorney for many years. Until now, I'd never had any reason to question him. I certainly owed him the benefit of the doubt.

"Bills, if you didn't bring that evidence to the lab," I said, "then I need to know who did and why Jim Taylor thinks it was you."

Bills paused for a second before answering.

"My wife and I are having dinner at the Cardinal tonight," Bills said. "If you go to the bar there at seven o'clock, I'll have some answers for you."

Since I was planning to eat there anyway, it seemed I had nothing to lose. I agreed to meet him. We both hung up.

About a minute later, Dom came out of the diner and hopped into the truck. He had a toothpick in his mouth.

"You call Bills?" he asked.

"Yeah," I answered sullenly.

Dom waited for a few seconds, expecting me to offer more. I said nothing. Finally, he could wait no longer.

"Well, what the fuck did he say?" Dom shouted.

I told him the details of my brief conversation with Bills.

"So, he'll give you your answers tonight," Dom said cheerily.

When I didn't reply, Dom spoke again.

"Trust me," Dom insisted. "Bills always comes through. He's as right as rain."

"Like John Hardy?" I asked sarcastically.

"You bet your ass," Dom answered immediately. "I've been in law enforcement for a long fucking time, kid. One thing I know for sure is that there are two kinds of people in this world – honest and dishonest. John Hardy and Roger Billingsley are good, honest people. Bills didn't lie to you and John Hardy didn't kill that scumbag."

I said nothing, but Dom's words had struck a nerve. I knew in my heart that he was probably right. My brain just seemed to be lagging behind. In a few hours though, I hoped to know the truth once and for all.

CHAPTER SIXTEEN

I had Dom drive me to my office. He pulled in, stopped by the rear entrance to the office, and let me out. I was almost to the door when Dom called out to me. He had his driver's window down and was leaning slightly out.

"I'll come by first thing tomorrow morning with whatever I can find on the Lawsons," he shouted.

"Keep your cell on," I shouted back. "I'll call you if I learn anything more."

"Copy that," he replied, before putting his truck in reverse and backing out of the lot. As he turned out on to the street, he turned on his radio. As he shifted to drive and accelerated away, I could hear "Thank God I'm a Country Boy" blasting through his open window.

I'm certainly not a fan of that kind of music, but I found myself singing along as I walked into my office. I hadn't gotten three or four steps inside when Casey's voice ran out.

"He ain't here yet, Mr. Wonderful," she bellowed, before realizing to her dismay that it was me, not Dom. She recovered very quickly.

"He's got you singing that crap now?" she demanded. "Bad enough hearing you play that Elvis music."

Casey never liked any of the music I liked, especially not Elvis Presley. I was a big fan of him and Frank Sinatra. Often, I played their music while I worked.

"You don't like the King, momma?" I asked in a very poor imitation of Elvis.

"The King is dead," she replied coldly.

I walked past her and started up the stairs to the kitchen to get some coffee. As I did, I said, "Well, I guess I'll just have to start singing Dom's music then."

"Long live the King," she shouted after me, causing both of us to burst out laughing. I could always count on Casey to lift my spirits.

For the next hour or so, I went through several of my files. Though Casey had cleared my calendar for the week, I did have a few cases coming up that needed my attention.

I was hoping that looking at different files and taking a brief break from the Hardy case might clear my mind. Sometimes, the best thing for a case is to do nothing. Then, when you come back to it, your mind seems fresh and picks up details you previously missed.

I was about to go back to the Hardy file when Casey buzzed me.

"Connor, it's a quarter after three," she announced. "Time to teach those kids how to kick ass."

That was how Casey always described my judo class. I had stopped correcting her weeks ago. It wasn't worth the battle. I just thanked her instead.

I took my files on the Hardy case with me and headed for the parking lot. As always, Casey had something to say as I left.

"Remind me to play you some real music," she offered.

"I did it my way," I sang in reply.

I could hear Casey groaning in mock suffering as I closed the door.

I drove straight to the dojo. It was already open and the kids were stretching in anticipation of class. Mr. Ito stood at the back of the room with his thumbs stuck into his faded red and white belt, signaling his status as a master.

I kicked off my shoes and walked to the back to change into my judo gi and belt. When I returned, Mr. Ito already had the children lined up to start the class. He always was extremely efficient.

As promised, I taught the kids the new throw I mentioned just two days earlier. First, I demonstrated the basic movements. Then, so the children could see how effective the move could be, I asked Mr. Ito to throw me with the technique.

He came forward and we bowed to each other. I took several steps back then charged at him. Ito caught hold of my lapel and sleeve and pulled forward and upward as he pivoted to my left side. Then, just as my right foot was about to hit the mat, he blocked me at the ankle with the sole of his foot. My ankle became the fulcrum of the throw and I flipped high in the air, landing with a resounding thud.

Several of the students inhaled sharply at the suddenness of the throw, while others giggled or commented at how cool the move had been. I got back to my feet and bowed to Mr. Ito.

Then, we paired up the kids to practice fitting in for the technique. I gave them strict instructions not to actually throw their partner yet. Most followed my order, though not all.

Toward the end of class, I matched up three pairs of students for sparring or randori. I let them battle one another for three minutes, each trying to throw the other. Then, I switched in three new pairs for another round. We did four rounds in total, and I was pleased to see three kids try the new throw. One even partially succeeded with it.

When class was over, I acknowledged their hard work and we bowed out.

As always, each of the children thanked Mr. Ito and me as they left. I remember when I first started the kids' class, nearly every student had to be coaxed by their parents to say thank you. Now, the children went out of their way to do so. It was very satisfying to see them grow and mature.

After the last of my students left, I changed back into my street clothes. Then, I did the paperwork necessary for attendance and future promotions of my students. I had just finished when Mr. Ito sat down next to me and cleared his throat.

I knew from years of being his student that when he cleared his throat in that way, he had something to say. I sat down in the chair next to him and waited for him to speak.

"Connor, I understand you were arrested last night?" he asked.

"I went down to the police station, but I wasn't arrested," I replied.

Mr. Ito nodded his head thoughtfully.

"One of my friends on the force tells me you fought three people," he said calmly. "Tell me about it."

I told him about the incident in Mrs. Edwards' backyard. He listened without comment until I described how Moose Whitfield's finger broke when I took away the gun. I was very surprised when Mr. Ito started to chuckle.

"You find this funny, Sensei?" I asked.

"No, no, you don't understand," he said. "You did the technique incorrectly."

"I took the gun away from him," I insisted, shocked at his claim.

"No," he said defiantly. "When the technique is done correctly, the trigger finger is supposed to come completely off."

He saw the look on my face when I heard his words. Whatever expression I had obviously amused him. He leaned his head back and laughed loudly.

"You always were so gullible," he said through his laughter.

When he finally stopped laughing, he said, "The point of the technique is to take away the gun without getting shot. You did that. To my knowledge, you are my first student ever forced to take away a gun. Well done."

"Thank you, Sensei." I said. Even as an adult, with a judo class of my own, it was always gratifying to receive praise from Mr. Ito, especially since he didn't do so very often.

"In the future, you need to be careful," he said, his face becoming very serious. "You are one of the best students I ever had. You have grown into a good man and an excellent martial artist."

"But?" I thought to myself, knowing full well that one was coming.

"But," he continued, "you cannot successfully take on two or three people at a time and expect to always win. You rushed in too quickly and put yourself in a position where you could have been killed."

"I realize that, Sensei," I answered. "That very thought occurred to me when he pulled the gun."

Ito nodded. Then he pointed at my head and said, "Remember, *that* is the best weapon in any situation."

I waited to see if he intended to say anything more. After a moment, he stood up and headed for the exit. When he got to the door, he looked back.

"You coming tomorrow night?" he asked.

"Yes, Sensei," I answered. "I'll cover tomorrow since you took last night for me."

"Nonsense," he said with a smile. "We'll cover it together."

After Mr. Ito left, I finished closing the dojo. I still had ninety minutes until I was supposed to meet Bills. So, I drove home and changed out of my suit. I put on jeans and a blue Oxford button-down shirt. I exchanged my dress shoes for an old, comfortable pair of sneakers.

As I was getting ready to leave, I noticed the red button flashing on my answering machine. I pressed the button and was pleased to hear Becky's cheerful voice.

"Hey, it's me. I'm working tonight, but have tomorrow off. How about we do lunch or better yet... a late supper. Call me."

Hearing her voice was always a pick-me-up. I wanted to talk to her right away, but I knew she would be working now. I called her cell anyway. It went straight to voicemail without ringing.

"Got your message," I started, "call me when you're done with work. We'll do lunch. Uhhh, see you soon."

I clicked off the phone and just shook my head in frustration. "We'll do lunch?" How lame was that? It was a miracle Becky even gave a geek like me the time of day, I thought to myself.

I thought of leaving a second message, but figured I'd just make it worse. So, I left my house and drove straight to The Cardinal and parked right out front.

Eddie was sitting in his usual place behind the bar and saw me as soon as I walked in. He had a huge smile on his face. I realized suddenly that he must have heard about the fight with the three punks. I braced myself for what I knew was coming.

"Ladies and gentlemen," Eddie shouted, his voice like a ring announcer, "the winner and still *champeen*, Con.... nor Club... ber Phe... lan!"

139

To further his comic routine—and my embarrassment—Eddie made a sound like a roaring crowd.

I walked over to the bar and sat down. Though I felt like every eye in the place was on me, I only noticed one old lady staring. She seemed more annoyed at Eddie than impressed with me.

"So," I said in an almost defeated tone, "You heard about the fight?"

"Are you kidding?" he asked. "This place is a big hangout for cops. I give them half-off on beer. Good for security."

"Can't argue with that," I said, starting to laugh. "But who told you?"

"Who didn't tell me," he replied. "Just about every cop who came in last night talked about it. They were seriously fucking impressed. Said you took that dirtbag's finger right off his fucking hand."

"Not completely off," I said, remembering Mr. Ito's words. "It was still hanging on when I saw it."

"Come on, man," Eddie said, rolling his eyes. "You could never be a promoter or a hype-man. The cops say you ripped off his finger. Don't ruin your image by telling people the finger was only partially off."

I smiled. "I did kind of fuck him up," I admitted.

"Yes!" Eddie shouted. "Much better. You're the man!"

Eddie reached under the bar and pulled out a small wooden box.

"I got something special for us to celebrate," he said. "It was given to me as a gift by my brother, Marty."

Marty Astorino, Eddie's older brother, lived in California and was a multi-millionaire. He owned an extremely successful company that developed computer software for the federal government.

Whenever he was in town, which was usually just for

Christmas, he made a big display of being unable to discuss the details of his company. He always called it "hush-hush". Whatever the nature of his software, there was no questioning its value. Marty always carried thick wads of cash and spent it like a drunken sailor. He also frequently sent his brother expensive gifts.

Whatever was in the small wooden box was certainly very good and very expensive.

Eddie opened the box and pulled out a bottle with amber liquid. He handed it to me. It was Midleton Very Rare, 30th Anniversary, Pearl Edition. I had heard of this brand of Irish whiskey. Every year, a limited number of bottles of Midleton were released. But this one was special. There had only ever been 117 bottles produced and they were obscenely priced.

"Can you believe it? Eddie said. "Marty had this shipped to me. The receipt was still in the package. That bottle and the wooden box it came in cost fifteen grand."

Without another word, I handed the bottle back to Eddie slowly and carefully. I was very relieved when it was no longer in my hands. If I had dropped it and fifteen thousand dollars' worth of whiskey poured on to the floor, I might have cried.

Eddie put the bottle on bar and put the box next to it.

"In honor of you kicking Moose Whitfield's ass, let's have a shot," he said forcefully.

"You sure you want to open it just for that?" I asked.

"I've been looking any excuse to crack this baby open," he said. "I figure if it costs fifteen grand, it must be fucking magnificent."

He pulled two glasses from under the bar and placed them next to the whiskey bottle. Then, he grabbed the top of the bottle, twisted it, and the cork came out with its distinctive sound. He poured two fingers worth in each glass. Then, he returned the cork to the bottle and placed the bottle gently into the wooden box. He closed the box and put it back under the counter.

He slid one of the glasses over to me and picked up the other. He raised it and contemplated the proper toast. When a sly smile crossed his lips, I knew he had one.

"My friend," he announced in his most sacred voice. "May you die in bed at the age of 106 at the hands of a jealous husband."

We clinked our glasses together and drank. I couldn't say it was worth fifteen thousand dollars, but I could say it was the best whiskey I had ever tasted. It was a mixture of sweet and spice, and was smooth as glass.

"Wow," Eddie said, his eyes wide with pleasure. "That is fucking awesome."

I couldn't disagree. I was about to take a second sip when I felt a large hand on my right shoulder. I turned to look. It was Roger Billingsley.

CHAPTER SEVENTEEN

"Could you give us a minute, Eddie," Bills said, as he sat down on the stool next to me.

Eddie nodded and gulped down the rest of his whiskey. It seemed a shame to gulp such wonderful whiskey when such nectar should have been savored.

After Eddie had left, Bills swiveled on his stool and looked at me directly.

"Connor, I completely understand why you think I lied to you," he began. "Chief Taylor told you what he was told by the lab. He didn't lie either."

"Bills, how can both be true?" I asked.

Bills held up one of his catcher-mitt hands to silence me.

"Just let me explain," he pressed.

I nodded my acquiescence, and he continued.

"I called the lab earlier today. They insist their records show that I dropped off the hair sample for analysis. So, I went down there myself. I spoke to the head of the lab, a man I've known for twenty-five years. The two of us went to the office and spoke with the woman who wrote their reports."

I was listening intently, but took another sip of my whiskey. Bills waited until I swallowed to continue his story.

"The woman actually had the nerve to say that I was not Roger Billingsley," he continued.

Now, I was intrigued.

"You mean somebody else signed it in under your name?" I asked incredulously.

"That's right," Bills said.

I felt a sense of great relief. There aren't many things in this world a person can rely on. Thinking Bills had gone bad had been a real shock. I was pleased to hear that it might not be so.

"Anyway," Bills pushed on, "based on the description of the man she gave, I felt I had a pretty good idea who it was."

"And," I interjected anxiously, "who was it?"

Bills shot me a look that expressed his desire quite clearly that he wanted me to stop talking. So, I did. He was going to tell the story his way and his way only.

"So, I went back to the D.A.'s Office and took a look in the Gilbert Russell murder file," the big man continued. "I confirmed my suspicions when I found these."

From inside the left lapel of his sport coat, Bills pulled out a packet of five or six documents folded vertically down the middle. He placed them on the bar and slid them over to me.

I took them and started to unfold them. Bills immediately put his hand over mine, causing my hand to completely disappear from sight.

"Not here," he insisted. "Bring them to your home or to your office and read them there. Show them to no one. If Worthington finds out that I gave you these, I could lose my job and my pension."

"Then, why are you giving them to me?" I asked, immediately regretting the question as I realized what the answer was. Bills was doing this because he felt it was the right thing to do. Bills had dedicated his life to law and order. His job had always been to put away the bad guys, but the right way.

Out of respect for his wishes, and to show my acceptance of his explanation, I folded the papers a second time and put them in my back pocket.

Bills nodded his approval. Then, he took a deep breath and spoke again.

"Have you ever heard of Officer Paul Brubaker?" he asked.

"No," I answered. "Should I have?"

"I wasn't sure you would have," Bills said. "He started with the Rockfield Police Department a few years after you left the D.A.'s office. Let's just say he is not the most trustworthy police officer."

My mind was racing. This was a wrinkle I did not expect.

"He's a bad cop?" I asked, slightly too loudly.

Bills immediately put a finger to his lips and shushed me.

"Not something to talk about here," he insisted. "Talk to Dom. He knows Brubaker and can tell you all about him."

Bills stood up and started back into the main part of the restaurant.

"Hey, Bills," I said, getting his attention. "I'm sorry I doubted you, old man."

It's fine," Bills said, smiling slightly. "You young kids have to learn somehow."

We both laughed.

"Just do me a favor," Bills said.

"Name it."

"Catch the real killer," Bills said, "and clear the judge's name."

"Count on it," I said.

Bills smiled and walked through the doorway and back to his table.

I turned back to the bar and finished the last of my whiskey.

My glass had barely clinked back on the counter when Eddie returned with a bottle of Glendalough, my usual.

I waved him off. "Not tonight, Eddie," I said. "I have work to do."

I reached into my pocket and pulled out a one-hundred-dollar bill. I handed it to Eddie. He looked almost offended.

"What's this?" he asked. "That glass of whiskey was on the house."

"I know that, Eddie," I said. "I'm buying dinner for Bills and his wife. That should cover the meal and tip, right?"

"With quite a bit to spare," Eddie replied.

"Would the amount to spare cover a glass of Midleton Very Rare for Bills?" I asked.

Eddie smiled in understanding.

"No," he said. "but Bills is good people. He usually drinks brandy, but I think he'll make an exception."

I shook Eddie's hand and left. As the door closed behind me, I heard his voice shout out.

"Don't let the fuckers get you down, Clubber!"

I decided right then and there that I was going to follow Eddie's advice. This case had gotten into my head. It was time to fight back and solve it.

I drove straight home. When I got there, I grabbed a cold beer. I took the beer and papers Bills had given me out to the patio. I lit a fire in the fire pit, and sat down in my preferred chair and began to drink and read.

The documents were very straightforward. They showed that Patrolman Paul Brubaker had gone to the morgue on a hunch and examined the body of Gilbert Russell. Though prior police technicians had found nothing, Brubaker found four hairs on Russell's shirt collar. He collected them and brought them directly to the lab.

There was no mention of using Roger Billingsley's name at

the lab. Brubaker's reports stated clearly that it was Brubaker himself who had submitted the evidence.

I set the papers down on the table in front of my chair. I picked up my beer and thought as I drank.

Obviously, using Billingsley's name had been a ruse. There were only two reasons to do that. The first was to hide Brubaker's identity. The second was in case anyone called the lab. Once anyone in law enforcement, or even on the defense side, heard the name Billingsley, they would have no doubts about the veracity of the evidence. It had worked on me at first.

Fortunately, Jim Taylor had suspected something was afoot and told me. I eventually called Bills and let him in on the deception.

The question burning in my mind was why did Brubaker involve himself in this case? Bills had not wanted to talk about Brubaker in public. All he was willing to say was that Brubaker was "not the most trustworthy police officer."

To answer my question, I needed to know more about this mysterious not-so-honest police officer. So, I pulled out my cell phone and called Dom.

"What's up, Connor," Dom answered, "You got something?"

"I sure do, boss," I said.

I told Dom all about my meeting with Bills. I left out the part about the great whiskey. I knew if I mentioned that, Dom would lose his focus for at least five to ten minutes.

Dom listened quietly until I said the name Brubaker. That got a reaction.

"Son of a bitch," Dom grunted. "That fucker is all we need."

"Hang on, Dom," I interrupted. "There's more."

I then read the reports to Dom that Bills had given me. When I finished reading, I set them back down on the table.

"So, tell me about this Brubaker character," I said.

"Paul Brubaker has been on the job for about five or six

years," Dom replied. "He's still on patrol because the brass have no intention of ever making him a sergeant."

"Because he's dirty?" I asked.

"Filthy," Dom said with a tone of disgust. "He brings in drug arrests like crazy. They all have the same set of facts. He claims he searches the suspect before putting them in the back of his patrol car. Then, when he gets to the station, he searches the backseat and miraculously finds a bump of crack, a deck of heroin, or a small bag of grass."

"Are you shitting me?" I asked. I could not believe someone could keep getting away with that.

"No, straight shit, pal," Dom insisted. "They can never prove he planted the stuff, and he always picks people with a long criminal record who have zero credibility. They scream that Brubaker planted it, but who's going to believe them?"

"So they just let this garbage continue?" I asked.

"They can't fire him without evidence," Dom said. "What they do is make sure as much as possible that he is never on duty alone. If he does make a questionable arrest, they dump the case quickly. Usually, the mutt is out within twenty-four hours to a week at most."

"Does he have a beef against John Hardy?"

"Sure does," Dom said. "Hardy was one of the first to meet with Chief Taylor about it. He didn't like seeing the same facts over and over again. Taylor suspended Brubaker for a week while they investigated."

"They find anything?" I asked.

"All they could get were the statements from the people he busted," Dom replied. "That wasn't enough to do anything. They had to let Brubaker back on the job and his record was cleared."

"Anything else?" I wondered.

"Not that I know of," Dom admitted. "But at least we have

something now. The evidence was found by a highly questionable officer who wasn't supposed to be on the case."

As Dom was speaking, I realized a problem with the entire scenario.

"Dom, we will have same issue that Chief Taylor had," I offered.

"What do you mean?" Dom asked in a surprised tone.

"Brubaker will deny it, right?"

"Sure as shit," Dom agreed.

"And all we have is John Hardy's word against him," I said. "A police officer against someone accused of murder. What are we going to do, put those credible drug users that Brubaker arrested on the stand?"

Dom was silent as he thought.

"What about Bills?" I offered hopefully. "Bills would be a great witness."

Although Dom was right about Bills, he was not seeing the entire picture.

"Dom, the jury will believe Bills, but think about what his testimony will be," I said, trying to remain calm.

"He'll tell them that he wasn't the one who brought the sample to the lab," Dom protested. Isn't that good enough to—"

"All it means," I interrupted, "is that the lab got the name wrong. It doesn't offer anything about Brubaker finding the hair on Russell's shirt."

Dom went silent.

"You understand now?" I asked.

"Fuck," Dom mumbled dejectedly. "So, what *do* we have?"

"It's still a good lead," I offered. "It's more than enough to support our theory of the evidence being planted."

"But, you just said—"

"I know what I just said," I interjected forcefully. "It's a start. I'm just going to have to have a heart-to-heart conversation with Officer Brubaker."

"Hold on a minute," Dom warned. "That may not be as easy as you think."

"I know how to talk to police officers," I insisted.

"Cut the shit," Dom implored. "I know you, and I know Brubaker. You'll confront him and you'll intentionally piss him off so he takes a poke at you."

"So what?" I asked. "If he does attack me, I can handle him and get some answers."

"I'm not sure you can," Dom replied.

"If he's a big guy or a tough guy, you know that's not a problem for me," I said defensively.

"No, you don't understand," Dom said more forcefully.

"Explain it to me, then."

"Paul Brubaker is not only a dirty cop," Dom said, "he's also a high-level black belt in Tae Kwon Do. He won some State level championship some years ago."

That certainly changed things. Brubaker might very well be a match for me. Tae Kwon Do or Korean Karate is very different than judo. It involves fast paced kicks and kicks to the head. When done by a master, the kicks could be deadly.

I thought for a few seconds before responding.

"Dom, forget about getting the background on the Lawsons," I said. "Instead, get me anything you can on Brubaker, especially on his martial arts background."

"Connor, you're really going to fight this guy?" Dom asked in a tone dripping with concern.

"If I have to," I answered. "I doubted John Hardy and then I doubted Bills. The only way I can clear Hardy's name and keep my promise to Bills is to confront Brubaker."

"Let me go with you," Dom offered. "My Sweet Lorraine can handle him."

Lorraine is the name Dom gave his Colt .45.

I laughed.

"Moose Whitfield thought his gun was enough," I said. "Look what happened to him."

I meant the comment as a joke, but Dom wasn't laughing.

"Connor, this guy is bad ass," Dom pressed. "Once, a suspect attacked Brubaker. He ended up in the hospital for weeks with broken ribs on both sides of his body. Don't take this guy cheap."

"I won't Dom," I said, trying to reassure him. "Just get me the background on him and we'll meet at my office tomorrow first thing. I promise I won't talk to Brubaker until after we talk. Fair enough?"

"Fair enough," Dom conceded.

We ended the call and I sat out on the patio for a long time just staring into the fire. I was going to have to confront Brubaker. If things turned ugly, I just hoped I was good enough.

CHAPTER EIGHTEEN

When I awoke the next morning, I was very surprised at
how soundly I had slept. As I'd gotten ready for bed,
my thoughts were soundly on Brubaker and the fight that was
likely coming. I'd expected that my entire night would be spent
plotting strategies to counter his kicks. Instead, I fell asleep
almost the moment my head had hit the pillow.

That day, I opted against wearing a suit. I had no court
appearances scheduled, so I went casual instead. I chose a loose-
fitting pair of dark-colored khakis, a polo shirt of almost the same
boring color, and a light jacket.

I made sure to take the documents Bills had given me and I
stuffed them into the jacket. I also packed a clean gi along with
my belt. I still planned to teach class that night. I also figured I
could use the class to warm up and to get some advice from
Mr. Ito.

Just before I left, I noticed the answering machine blinking.
I hadn't checked it the night before. The message was from
Becky.

"Got your message," she said, in a voice almost too sexy to be real. "Lunch sounds perfect. Meet me at noon at the usual place. Bye."

The usual place was a small deli about three blocks from my office that served great pastrami sandwiches. Well, I thought to myself, at least I have something to look forward to before I face off with Brubaker.

I had been so preoccupied with my thoughts that I neglected to pick up coffee on the way to the office. Fortunately, Casey had a mug waiting for me on my desk. I was amused that she always had coffee for me. I never asked her to get it. I figured Casey would find it insulting and demeaning, but she had started doing it a few weeks after she started working with me. We never discussed it. I just figured I would leave it up to her. If she chose not to get the coffee, I was more than capable of getting it myself.

I sat at my desk and started drinking. As always, it was made just the way I like it. As I sipped, I added the documents from Bills into the main Hardy file.

I was about three-quarters done with my coffee when I heard a familiar voice.

"Hey, beautiful, is he in?"

This was followed by Casey's sarcastic bellowing.

"Mr. Wonderful to see you, Connor."

"Send him in," I chimed, hoping that there would be no griping back and forth between them today. No such luck.

"Young lady, I know I'm wonderful and all that, but do you have to always announce me that way?" Dom asked.

I waited for Casey's answer. Dom always pushed her buttons and he almost always lost. Casey has one of the quickest minds I have ever seen.

"You're right," she said serenely. "I apologize. I should be more accurate."

I nearly spat out my coffee when I heard her apologize. I

quickly swallowed what was left in my mouth as I sensed the other shoe was about to drop, and I did not want to choke.

"Mr. Phelan?" Casey announced sweetly, "Mr. Not-So-Wonderful to see you."

"Now, see here young lady," Dom roared, "I've had about enough of you and your—"

"Dom!" I shouted. "Just come in here please. We don't have time for this today."

Dom did as I asked, though he grumbled the entire way under his breath.

I looked over at my open door and could see Casey sitting at her desk. She smiled like the cat that swallowed the canary. I stood up and walked to my door. Trying not to laugh, I made a *tsk tsk* motion with my fingers.

Casey pointed her fingers at her chest and raised her eyebrows in a "Who me?" gesture. I closed the door and went back to my chair.

"You need to do something about that wiseass," Dom demanded.

"I've told you many times that if you poke the bear, you're going to get bit," I admonished.

He opened his mouth to speak, but I beat him to it.

"What do you have on Brubaker?" I asked.

Dom handed me a thin file. Inside were printouts from the New York State Tae Kwon Do Federation and a few news articles showing that Paul Brubaker was a three-time state sparring champion. His most recent title had been won four years ago and recorded his rank as 3rd dan or third-degree black belt.

"Did he stop competing four years ago?" I asked.

Dom laughed, but without any sense of humor. "Look at the last news article," he said grimly.

I flipped to the last page. It was an article from the *Rockfield*

Tribune from slightly more than three years ago. The headline read:

Local martial artist arrested after fight with instructor

There were pictures of two men identified as Paul Brubaker and Ryong Gee.

I started reading the article, but Dom decided not to wait.

"I was on that case," Dom said. "Seems that Brubaker and Master Ryong Gee got into a wild argument."

"What about?" I asked, looking up from the article.

"Mr. Gee said it had to do with his refusal to promote him to the next level," Dom said. "Brubaker felt he earned it by winning the tournament three straight years, but Master Gee refused to give it to him. Said this rank would make him a Master in some schools, but he felt Brubaker had a bad attitude."

"Brubaker got into a fight with his instructor?" I asked.

"Give the man a cigar," Dom said sarcastically. "Brubaker lost his temper and attacked Master Gee. When the first officers arrived on the scene, they saw both men in front of the studio. Brubaker throwing kicks and punches like crazy. Fortunately, Brubaker didn't fight the cops. He stopped and allowed himself to be cuffed."

"Was Ryong Gi arrested?" I asked.

"No," Dom answered. "The officers said he was blocking everything Brubaker threw at him, but never fought back."

Obviously, he was a good teacher, I thought to myself. He defended himself, but would not fight his student. Obviously, he was an honorable man.

"Whatever happened to the charges against Brubaker?" I asked. "How did he make the force with a criminal conviction?"

"There was no conviction," Dom replied. "Ryong Gee agreed to drop all charges, so long as Brubaker never returned to his class."

"At least now I can talk to Master Gee and get some advice on how to defeat Brubaker."

"Not likely," Dom replied. "He died about a year ago."

"One step forward and two steps back," I mumbled.

"Sorry, pal," Dom said quietly.

It was time to change the subject.

"Is there some place Brubaker hangs out when he's off duty?" I asked. "The last thing I want to do is risk a confrontation when he's in uniform."

"And armed," Dom added.

That was certainly true. I was in no hurry to disarm another attacker with a gun. Once was more than enough.

"He has a side job," Dom said. "He works evenings Thursday through Saturday at the Queen of Hearts."

"The strip club?" I asked.

"The very same," Dom said with a big smile. "Tonight is *Thirsty Thursday*. The first one hundred customers get fifty percent off beer and lap dances."

I was tempted to ask him if there were other specials, but I decided I didn't want to know. I had been to strip clubs when I was in law school. I hadn't been in one since my bachelor party. Once I was married, I just didn't see the point.

"What time do they open?" I asked.

"Oh, you want make sure you're in the first hundred?" Dom asked. "Looking for a special dance?"

"No," I said with a scowl. "I figure it will not be as busy in the early hours, even with the special. When I confront Brubaker, I want as few people around as possible."

"You sure you don't want me to come along as backup?" Dom offered. "This guy is not just some punk. He's bad ass."

"Thank you," I said, "but I think I should do this alone."

"Well, good luck," Dom said, as he stood up. "They open at nine."

I walked Dom out to his car. As we passed by Casey, I ran my fingers under my throat as a sign for her not to say anything. Mercifully, she did not.

When it finally reached noon, I found myself sitting with Becky and munching on a thick and juicy pastrami on rye. The sandwich was great, but the best part was seeing Becky again.

She looked beautiful. She was dressed in faded blue jeans and a white top. She also wore a faded jean jacket. Her hair was back in a ponytail. When she first walked in, she looked so good, I thought my heart might beat through my chest.

The only thing missing right now was her smile. I'd seen it when she first came in, but it disappeared completely after I'd told her about Paul Brubaker. Part of me wanted to keep it from her so she wouldn't worry. I ended up telling her because I felt that if I started keeping secrets from her now, it could screw up our relationship. Things were going very well, and my goal was not to fuck it up.

"Connor," she said, her concern evident, why do you have to fight this guy?"

I'm not going there with the intention to fight him," I offered in defense. "I just want to ask him some questions."

"Oh, cow cookies," she said, stamping her foot. "You know damn well that he's not going to answer. He's going to attack you and then you fight."

"You know I can take care of myself," I insisted. "Hell, I'm teaching you."

She started to speak, but I pressed my perceived advantage.

"You didn't think I could take your giant gorilla of an ex-husband, did you?"

"That's not the same thing," she nearly shouted. "He was

big and tough, but he wasn't trained like you. This guy is trained. He's a third-degree black belt. You're only second degree."

"Just because someone has a higher rank," I argued, "doesn't mean they are automatically better. Besides, he's high ranked in Tae Kwon Do. Judo is completely different."

"You said his style involves kicks that are really fast," Becky pressed. "You said the kicks to the head can be lethal."

I started to say something, but saw a tear begin to fall from her right eye. As it made its way down her cheek, I reached out with my finger and gently stopped its descent.

"It's okay, Becky," I said softly. "I'll be fine. I'll be back later tonight and we can celebrate my victory."

"I hope so," she answered, not sounding at all convinced.

I wished I was as confident inside as I had just pretended to be for Becky. I considered following my previous thoughts of complete honesty, but I just couldn't do it. If I told Becky how nervous I really was and told her that there was a real chance that I might end up in the hospital, she would come apart and cry uncontrollably. So, I kept it to myself.

In truth, seeing her cry would hurt a hell of a lot more than Brubaker smashing my ribs.

We finished our lunch and I walked Becky to her car. I opened the door for her, but she just stood there for a moment. Then she put her arms around me and hugged me close. She put her lips against my ear and whispered.

"I'm sorry to be such a downer, but I just don't want to see you get hurt," she said.

"Becky, I..."

She squeezed the grip of her hug tighter and I took the hint and stopped talking.

"I worry about you because I love you more than I have loved anyone else in my entire life."

These words hit home. I loved her too. I started to consider something that six months ago would have been almost sacrilegious to me. I not only loved her, but I felt that I too loved Becky more than anyone else, even my late wife, Melissa. However, this was not something I could consider right now.

I pulled back a little so I could see her face. I placed my left hand on her cheek and gently caressed it.

"I love you too, Becky."

She leaned in and kissed me. Now, there was no doubt about how I felt. I continued to kiss her.

CHAPTER NINETEEN

That afternoon, I stopped by Judge Hardy's home. When he answered the door, his face lit right up. For an extrovert personality like his, being unable to leave your home and converse with other people was sheer torture. Even though I was certain he would prefer his current circumstance to being in jail, I also knew he was suffering emotionally.

"Connor, my boy," he said happily, holding the door open wide. "Come on in."

I followed him to his grandiose parlor, where we both took a seat. I filled him in on the latest developments, including Paul Brubaker.

"That lousy bastard," Hardy lamented, when I had finished. "Why would he target me?"

"Dom seems to think it has something to do with the meeting you had with Jim Taylor," I offered.

Hardy shook his head. "I find that hard to believe," he said.

"Well," I countered, "he was suspended for a week."

"He was eventually cleared," Hardy insisted. "Besides, it was Taylor who suspended him, not me. No, there's more going on here."

"I agree that his motive seems less than compelling," I said. "But, it is the first real break we've had."

"True enough," Hardy conceded.

Now, I had a much more difficult topic to broach.

"John," I started, "I owe you an apology."

Hardy smiled almost immediately. He had the look of a parent who just heard his or her toddler say something ridiculous.

"What the devil for?" he asked.

"I doubted you, John," I said. "When I learned that your DNA was found at the scene, I wondered..."

I paused, trying to find the right words.

"I thought that maybe... that perhaps you..."

"You thought I might have killed that low life," Hardy finished.

"Well, yeah," I admitted. "I didn't want to believe it. It was tearing me up inside."

Hardy laughed and put his hand on my shoulder.

"If I had been representing you, I probably would have thought the same thing," he said, surprising the hell out of me.

"But, John," I interrupted, "I actually thought you might be capable of murder."

"Connor, let's get right to the heart of it," Hardy said, in an almost cheery voice. "I'm just as capable of taking a life as you are. We're all human beings, my boy. We are emotional creatures that sometimes let our anger and our primitive rage get the better of us."

"But we don't run around hanging people," I interjected.

"No, we don't," Hardy acknowledged. "Son, I've been involved in the criminal justice system for over fifty years. In that time, I've seen people do some terrible things. One of my very first cases as a young assistant district attorney was the murder of a young woman. Before she was strangled, she had been stripped, tied up, and her behind whipped with a leather belt."

"Sounds like a pretty twisted killer," I replied.

"That's what we all thought," Hardy continued. "Turned out the killer was a man with whom she had been having an affair. Care to guess who he was?"

I shrugged.

"It was her own church minister," Hardy said. "He was supposed to be a man of God, someone you could trust. Instead, he was a sadistic killer."

"Odd, I never heard of that case," I said.

"That was from before you were even a gleam in your daddy's eye, Connor," Hardy answered. "The point is that we're all human beings capable of doing awful things. You followed the evidence and made a rational conclusion. Suspecting me of being the murderer doesn't make you immoral. It's the inner turmoil you went through that proves what a good man you really are."

I felt so relieved. On my way over, I worried about how John would react. I owed him the truth, but figured he would throw me out of his house when he heard it. His kind and understanding reaction lifted a heavy burden of guilt off my shoulders. Various words of gratitude raced through my head. Instead, I just stuck out my hand.

"Thanks, John," I said, as he shook my hand.

"So, what's next?" Hardy asked, changing the subject.

"I have to have a nice conversation with Paul Brubaker," I replied.

Hardy's face registered a look of concern.

"That may not be so easy," he offered.

"I know," I answered, "but I have no choice. He's not going to just admit in court that he planted evidence against you."

"I agree," Hardy said. "Just be careful. Brubaker is dangerous. He's a liar and as tough as nails."

We walked to the door. As I was leaving, I turned back to the judge.

"I'll see you tomorrow morning in court." I said.

"Yes, my preliminary hearing," Hardy replied. "You ready for it?"

"I'm as ready as you are," I said with a smile.

As he closed the front door, I heard Hardy reply with a slight chuckle, "Then we're screwed."

After driving off from Hardy's house, I stopped at a nearby McDonalds for a quick bite to eat. I ate lightly, just a plain hamburger, small order of fries, and a Diet Coke. I wasn't that hungry, and I planned on working out and later confronting Officer Brubaker. The last thing I needed was a heavy meal in my stomach.

At 6:45pm, I pulled up to the dojo. When I entered, Mr. Ito was already waiting for me. A couple of the adult students were warming up on the mats, including Becky. She smiled nervously when she saw me.

I had forgotten that she would be here. Obviously, my mind was on the upcoming confrontation with Brubaker. I winked at Becky as I walked past her toward the dressing room.

After I had changed into my judo gi and returned to the mats, I approached Mr. Ito.

"Sensei?" I said, getting his attention. "May I speak with you?"

Ito nodded and sat in the chair by the desk.

"Later tonight, I have to talk with someone and there's a good chance it will lead to a fight," I said.

Ito seemed confused.

"Connor, you have had fights before. You know how to defend yourself," he answered quietly.

"This one is different," I replied. "He's a third-degree black belt in Tae Kwon Do, not some drunk fool wildly throwing punches."

Ito just nodded again, but said nothing.

"I know you have experience and training in several styles. Is there any advice you can give me?" I asked. "Maybe a weakness in Tae Kwon Do?"

Ito shook his head.

"Tae Kwon Do is a martial art. So is judo and many others," he said. "It is not a question of which is better or worse."

He paused, but I said nothing. I knew from experience that he often paused for long moments in the middle of our conversations, to reflect thoroughly on the issues.

"A martial artist must adapt his style to the situation before him," he continued. "Remember, that your best weapon is never your hands or your feet. It is always your brain."

Without another word or giving me the opportunity to respond, he stood up and ordered everyone to line up for the start of class. I joined him at the front of the dojo. I had a lot of questions, but it was clear that my sensei had nothing further to say on the matter.

The workout was a good one. Since Ito was the highest rank present and since this was his usual night to teach, I deferred entirely to him. He worked the class very hard. There were no new techniques taught that night. Instead, we did drills over and over again that were designed to develop endurance and muscle memory.

Toward the end of class, Ito matched up students for randori. After three rounds, he ordered the class to sit against the wall.

"There will be one more round tonight," Ito said, "but not for you. I want all of you to watch."

He then turned to me and pointed directly in front of him.

"You will play me," he instructed.

I had not anticipated this. I had played against Ito many times as a student. I had never beaten him. But that was a long time ago. It had been many years since we faced off. Now, he was an old man. As I walked toward him, I decided I would take it easy on him. The last thing I wanted to do was embarrass him in front of the students.

After we bowed, we each took our grip and the contest began. We moved around, but neither of us attacked. We just shifted position. After about ten seconds, Ito moved for a basic right-sided shoulder throw. I shifted my hips to block. He immediately changed direction and threw me cleanly with the same technique, but to the left side. I was amazed at the speed the old man had demonstrated.

As I got up, Ito looked annoyed.

"Is that the best you can do?" he asked mockingly.

I was more than a little embarrassed. So, I went after him with every bit of strength, speed, and skill I could muster. Over the next five minutes, he blocked everything I did, seemingly with ease. Once or twice, I thought I had him. Each time, he made a subtle movement or shift and I found myself airborne.

To my annoyance, each time he slammed me to the mat, he repeated, "Is that the best you can do?"

I got up each time and went after him even harder. I was determined to throw him, but kept finding myself tossed like a rag doll. After I landed for the fifth or sixth time, Ito called an end to the round and ordered everyone to line up. I got back to my feet and bowed to him. I was dripping with sweat and breathing very heavily.

When everyone was in position, he addressed the class again.

"Does anyone know why I defeated Connor?" he asked.

None of the students had an answer. They had never seen me dominated like that before. So, I spoke.

"Because you are better than I am," I said, through my still-heavy breathing, causing the students to laugh nervously.

Ito smiled in satisfaction.

"True," he said, "but not exactly what I was looking for. Connor is younger than me, stronger than me, and faster than me. I am an old man, but still I defeated him. How? What was his mistake?"

He glanced around but found no answer from the students. Then, he looked to me. I also had no answer.

"Your best weapon is never your hands or your feet. It is always your brain," he said, staring at me strongly. "Connor was being respectful at first. He didn't want to embarrass his old sensei. After I threw him the first time, I ordered him to attack. He did. Each time I threw him, I mocked him. As Connor got angrier, he became reckless. His technique got sloppy and I countered him. His mistake was listening to me. He should have remained calm and adapted his technique to his situation."

He said nothing more. He merely turned to the front of the dojo signaling the start of the bowing ceremony that would end the class.

Within twenty minutes, the dojo was empty again, except for Becky, Mr. Ito, and myself. All three of us were back in our street clothes.

"Connor, do you want me to come with you tonight?" Mr. Ito offered.

"No, Sensei," I replied. "Thank you for offering, but I think it would be better if I went alone."

Ito nodded, but said nothing.

"Connor, if this Brubaker guy is as dangerous as you say," Becky said, her voice filled with concern, "maybe it would be better if you had backup."

"No," I said firmly. "I'll handle it."

"But, Connor," she pressed, "I don't want to see you—"

"I'll be fine," I insisted. As I left the dojo, I looked back and saw Becky. I could tell that my reassurance had not worked. She was still very nervous. So was I.

CHAPTER TWENTY

I arrived at the Queen of Hearts about five minutes before it was set to open. There were already about ten men waiting in line. I parked my Cherokee and waited. I felt it was much more prudent to wait for the anxious line to get inside before approaching Brubaker.

Eventually, the main door opened and an extremely large man came out. He was obviously a body builder. He wore jeans and an orange sleeveless shirt that showed off his impressive arms. His biceps were as big as my legs. The shirt was so tight around his chest, I expected he would burst through it like the Incredible Hulk. I prayed he was not Brubaker.

The enormous bouncer took his position at the head of the line and began checking IDs. After everyone had been admitted, the gigantic man pulled out a cigarette, lit it, and put it in his mouth. Then, he leaned against the building and blew out smoke.

I got out of the Cherokee and made my way to the entrance. As I did, I could hear music and men cheering from inside. Clearly, the show had started.

When I reached the door, the bouncer took a step toward me.

"ID please," he announced in a gruff voice.

"I'm not looking to go in," I said.

The man seemed confused for a second. Then, he regained whatever mental capacity he usually possessed.

"What the fuck do you want then?" he demanded.

"I'm looking for Paul Brubaker," I replied.

"What do you need him for?" he insisted.

"That's between him and me," I answered.

The bouncer eyed me suspiciously for a long moment before he spoke again.

"All right," he grunted, "wait here."

Without another word, he opened the door and disappeared inside.

Two minutes later, he returned. I was just about to ask him why he was alone, when a second man came out. He was slightly taller than me and slender. He had dark hair shaved into a crew cut on top and to the skin on the sides. He had a thick mustache and two days' growth on the rest of his face. Underneath an unzipped black jacket, he wore a tan polo shirt with matching khaki pants. I could tell that he was in good physical shape.

"You Brubaker?" I asked.

"Yeah," Brubaker replied, as he chewed casually on a toothpick. "What do you want?"

"My name is Connor Phelan," I said politely, "and I—"

"I know who you are," Brubaker interrupted. "Now, what the hell do you want?"

This was not getting off to a particularly good start, I thought to myself. Still, I needed to remain calm and hopefully prevent this conversation from developing into the fight I knew was probably coming.

"I want to talk to you about Judge John Hardy," I said.

"Got nothing to say about him," Brubaker sneered. "Now, maybe you ought to—"

"More specifically," I interjected, "I want to talk about the hair evidence you supposedly found."

Brubaker's eyes went wide and he took a step toward me. I moved my right foot back into a defensive stance in case he decided to attack.

"What do you mean *supposedly* found?" he shouted. "You calling me a liar?"

"We both know you didn't actually find any hair," I replied, trying with great difficulty to keep my voice calm. "I want to know why you planted that evidence against Hardy. What's your beef with him?"

Brubaker's face turned almost crimson and he took another step toward me. This time I held my ground. If, or more precisely when, this nice conversation turned violent, I needed to be closer to him so his wide kicks would be of limited use to him.

"I've got no beef with the judge," he snarled, "and I didn't plant any evidence. Not my fault the fucker's guilty."

"Hardy didn't kill Russell," I pressed.

"And neither did I!" Brubaker shouted.

"Did I say you did?" I yelled back. "I did not accuse you of murder. I accused you of planting evidence!"

Brubaker stepped even closer to me and looked directly into my eyes. He was so close I could smell the cigarettes and beer on his breath.

"You listen to me, you motherfucker," he growled. "I didn't plant a fucking thing. Get the hell out of here before I beat the shit out of you."

I took a deep breath. It was more to steady myself before I spoke again.

"I'm not leaving until I get the answers I want," I insisted.

Brubaker reached out with both hands, grabbed me by the shirt, and started pushing me backwards. I grabbed hold of his jacket and pulled him toward me. Then, while still pulling him toward me, I fell backwards, pivoted to my right, and extended my left leg in front of him.

Between his pushing and my falling backwards, enough momentum developed to cause Brubaker to flip over my left leg to the ground. I got back to my feet and was surprised to see that Brubaker was already standing. He must have rolled with my throw to a standing position.

Brubaker had dirt on his jacket and pants, but he did not seem injured at all. It had been a solid throw, but apparently not all that effective.

Brubaker smiled coldly. He seemed unconcerned and not at all worried about me. He just took a step back and turned casually to the huge bouncer who was again leaning against the building.

"Wait for me inside, Pee Wee," he ordered. "This won't take more than a minute or so."

I could not believe I did not burst out laughing when I heard him call that goliath "Pee Wee". However, it must have been his name, because he immediately tossed his cigarette to the ground and crushed it underfoot, before walking through the door and into the club.

As soon as the door closed, Brubaker threw a right roundhouse kick at my head. I ducked it and came forward so I could grab hold of him. Brubaker followed through with his momentum and spun into a reverse left back kick. It struck me a grazing blow on the front of my left shoulder.

Though he had not hit me flush, the kick was still strong enough to knock me down. I landed flat on my back. As I stood up, I realized that if he had connected fully with that kick, he likely would have broken at least two of my bones.

I approached Brubaker watching his movements very carefully. He feinted with his hands twice, each time seeing how I would react. I didn't move a muscle. Then, he came at me with a series of kicks aimed at my head. I was able to avoid all of them by either blocking or ducking.

The entire time, I was looking for any way to get my hands on him. I knew if I could make this a contest of grappling, I would have a distinct advantage. Brubaker seemed to know this as well. He kept close enough to throw kicks, but not so close that I could grab him.

I was sweating freely now. Brubaker was fast and his kicks were solid. Just blocking and dodging his attacks was wearing me out. I could not win this fight unless I got past his kicks. If I stayed at this distance, eventually one of his kicks would connect and my lights would go out.

Finally, he raised his leg for another kick. I came forward to get underneath it, but realized a second too late that I had made a major mistake. It had been a feint. When I came forward, he lowered his leg and pivoted his hips so that he was quickly back to a roundhouse kick position. He then snapped off a quick roundhouse kick that struck me in the face.

Stars exploded upon impact and I crumpled to the ground. I could taste the blood as it ran down my face. I struggled to regain my senses and get back to my feet. A powerful hand grabbed me by the shirt and lifted me slightly. As my vision came back, I saw Brubaker kneeling over me. He had his left hand holding up my head and his right fist was cocked back.

I considered fighting back, but decided against it. If I started punching or grappling from this position, it would probably end badly. My only chance was to follow Sensei Ito's advice. I had to remain calm and adapt to the situation. So, I remained limp as if barely conscious.

"Now, motherfucker," Brubaker roared, "I'm gonna fuck you up."

He wound up his fist even further and drove it down at me with all of his weight behind it. At the last possible second, I rolled to my right. Brubaker's fist missed me and slammed into the hard packed dirt of the parking lot. I heard bones in his hand break and Brubaker screamed in agony.

I immediately sat up and slammed my forearm and elbow into the side of his head. He grunted and starting slumping. I used my left arm to wrap-up and secure his right arm. Grabbing his leather jacket with my free hand and using my legs, I rolled him over so he was on his back and I was on top of him. I had his right arm wrapped so tightly, he had no chance of getting it free. He was effectively at my mercy. Brubaker threw punches with his left hand, but he was not able to land them effectively. He hit my right shoulder once. It hurt, but not enough to make me let go.

I knew I could hold Brubaker down on the ground indefinitely, but it would not get me the information I needed.

"Tell me why you planted that evidence, Brubaker!" I shouted.

His answer came quickly.

"Fuck you."

So much for that idea.

I released my grip on his jacket and brought my right hand loose. I lifted it has high as I could and smashed my elbow into Brubaker's nose. He grunted and his nose bled freely.

"Tell me what I want to know!" I shouted again.

He said nothing. He just kept trying to hit me or escape. I hit him again with my elbow.

"Tell me!"

I smashed his nose with my elbow for a third time. This time I felt it break. I also felt him go completely limp. He was knocked out. I waited a few seconds to make sure. Then, certain he was out and growing tired of his blood pouring onto me, I released my hold. He lay quietly on the ground.

I staggered to my feet. I could feel my jaw where he had kicked me. It hurt so badly, I thought he might have broken my jaw. I looked down and Brubaker was still on the ground. He was not moving.

Just great, I thought. I beat him, but got no information whatsoever.

"Holy shit."

Startled, I turned and saw that Pee Wee had returned. He looked at me and then looked at Brubaker. He seemed to consider his options for a moment. Then, without another sound, he went back into the Queen of Hearts.

I had taken two or three steps toward my car, when I heard something behind me. I looked and saw that Brubaker was getting back to his feet. His nose was still bleeding profusely and his hand looked purple and ugly. He was breathing heavily and his eyes showed hatred. He staggered toward me and went into a fighting stance.

"Enough, Brubaker," I said. "Just tell me what I want to know."

"Come on," he croaked, signaling me forward with his left hand.

"It's over," I replied. "Just tell me why you did it."

Brubaker shook his head and started toward me.

"Last chance," I cautioned.

He ignored my warning and attacked. He threw a right sidekick at me. It was not as fast or strong as it had been when we started. I stepped to my left and easily deflected his kick with my right arm. This made Brubaker lose his balance. I moved behind him and grabbed both of his shoulders. I pulled him back and dropped to my knee as I did. Brubaker slammed to the ground and I could hear the air come out of his lungs when he landed.

I grabbed his left wrist and pulled up. At the same time, I put my left foot under his ribs. I slid my right leg over his neck and sat down, trapping his arm between my legs. I leaned back and squeezed my knees together which hyperextended his elbow. Brubaker screamed.

"Tell me!" I shouted. "Don't make me snap your elbow."

When he did not reply, I squeezed my knees again, but slightly harder. Brubaker screamed again.

"All right. All right," he wailed.

I stopped squeezing my knees, but kept his arm tight.

"Well," I demanded. "Why did you do it?"

"I was paid to do it," he confessed.

"Who paid you?" I insisted, tightening my knees just slightly.

Brubaker hissed an answer that completely stunned me.

"It was Worthington."

CHAPTER TWENTY-ONE

I was so stunned by Brubaker's accusation, I let go completely of his arm. He rolled to his left and grabbed his elbow, pulling it close to his side. He made no attempt to stand or fight. He was beaten and he knew it. I stood and positioned myself close enough to speak with him, but far enough away that he couldn't kick me if he changed his mind.

"Tell me more," I demanded. "Why did Worthington want evidence planted?"

"No idea," he grunted. "He called me and told me he had a job for me. Said if I did it correctly and kept it quiet, it would be worth five grand and more."

"More?" I asked, uncertain what else that snake could offer besides money.

"He said that there will soon be an opening in his office for a Chief Investigator," Brubaker continued. "If I played ball, the job would be mine."

I couldn't believe what I was hearing. I knew the illustrious J. Robert Worthington was a sniveling coward. I also knew that he despised Judge Hardy. Hardy was a better man and a better district attorney. Worthington was incapable of living up to the local legend.

I never even considered that his hatred and jealousy went so far that he would try to frame him for murder. Then to add to his treachery, he planned to fire Bills. Did he know about Bills giving me information or was he just collateral damage from his plan? There was no way to know for sure.

Interestingly, though I never thought Worthington was capable of sinking so low, I found that I believed Brubaker completely. If Worthington wanted to get John Hardy, this was the perfect setup.

Hardy had made the foolish boast in open court that Gilbert Russell should be taken to the town square and hanged. That made him a suspect right away.

Also, Russell was universally hated and despised. Nobody in the entire county shed a tear on learning of his death. In fact, in the local gin mills, toasts were made to his death and in honor of the one who executed him. There would be no uprising over the failure to find the real murderer. Moreover, as Russell had no family, there were no grieving relatives demanding justice.

Brubaker had moved to a seated position. He still cradled his left arm against his body. I knew I had not broken his arm, but it had been stretched considerably. It would be immensely sore for several days.

Though I was able to accept Brubaker's confession of being bribed to frame John Hardy, there was still another, more serious question. Who actually killed Gilbert Russell?

"Did you kill Russell?" I asked Brubaker, as I glared down at him.

"No, way," he said immediately. "I planted the hair. That's it."

I stared at him intently trying to decide whether to believe him.

"Look," Brubaker said, a look of fear creeping into his eyes, "I don't mind fabricating some evidence now and then to make sure some guilty scumbags go to prison. I don't kill people in cold blood."

I believed him. Besides, Worthington was much too namby-pamby to have committed the murder himself. As for hiring someone to do it, I found that too difficult to accept. It seemed more likely to me that Worthington was just taking advantage of the opportunity. That fit his personality. Worthington was a conniving son of a bitch, but not a killer or someone who would hire one.

If I was right, then Brubaker wasn't going to lead me to the murderer. He would, however, be the key to acquitting Judge Hardy. That was my primary responsibility as his attorney. I needed to get as many details as I could from Brubaker now, before he had time to recover and try me again. I had barely beaten him this time. I wasn't anxious for a rematch.

"How did you get Hardy's hair in the first place?" I demanded. "Worthington give it to you?"

"That asshole?" Brubaker laughed. "He couldn't count to twenty-one unless he was naked."

"Then, where did you get it?"

Brubaker took a deep breath and stared at me hard. When he started speaking, I was confident that I was getting the straight story.

"Worthington told me he wanted Hardy set up for the murder," Brubaker said. "How to do it was left to me. So, since I do have some *experience* in such matters, I thought that forensic evidence would be easiest way."

"Go on," I pressed, anxious to hear the rest.

"So, later that evening, I went into the courthouse and to the judge's chambers," Brubaker resumed. "I knew he wouldn't be in there because there was a ceremony in the courtroom honoring the attorneys who died the previous year."

I recalled hearing about that meeting. I hadn't been able to attend this year, but had been there in years past. It was an annual event always done about the same time of year. Judge Hardy was always the guest of honor. He would call the court into session and recognize the President of the county bar association, who then read off the list of those attorneys who passed the previous year. There would be speeches and plaques awarded. The ceremony usually lasted about thirty minutes.

"While those attorneys blathered on," Brubaker said, "I went to the judge's chambers. It wasn't locked. I looked through his coat hoping to find a used tissue or handkerchief. I found nothing. But, when I looked in his hat, I found a lot of hair. The old coot is shedding like a furry dog. Since his hair is bright white, they stood out against the dark hat. I took as many as I could and stuck them in an evidence bag I brought."

I shook my head in amazement. It was a brilliant setup. That one of the hairs had a root made it all the easier. It allowed for the DNA test to come back quickly.

"Then to hide what you had done," I offered, "you submitted it to the lab under Roger Billingsley's name."

"No," he insisted. "That was Worthington's order. He said that he wanted to keep my involvement a secret until the trial."

That threw me for a second. Even at trial, I thought, eventually Brubaker's name would come up. Any defense attorney worth a damn would find out about Brubaker's reputation and use it against the prosecution. There was a reasonable chance that, with no other evidence, Hardy would be exonerated.

What was the point of all this? What did Worthington hope to gain?

Then, in a flash, I understood. Worthington didn't need

Hardy to be convicted for his plan to work. That would just be icing on the cake. John Hardy was up for reelection next year. The local parties would nominate their candidates in mid to late March, just five months away. Once indicted, Worthington could easily delay the trial that long.

When the party leaders got together, despite Hardy's popularity and money, they would be too scared of his potential conviction and the effect on their other candidates to nominate him for reelection. Party bosses from either major party were the most timid people in the world around election time. They would not hesitate to drop their support to protect their political backsides at a moment's notice.

With Hardy out of the way, Worthington would be the obvious choice to succeed him as county court judge. Once nominated and secured on the ballot, even if Hardy was later acquitted, he would still be through as judge. Worthington would finally follow his father's footsteps and be sworn in as a judge.

Worthington may have been a simpleton when it came to the law, but he was well schooled in the art of politics. It was a world of deception, back door deals, and betrayal; a world where Worthington was right at home.

I was still contemplating what a despicable piece of garbage Worthington was, when I was grabbed from behind and my arms held fast.

Pee Wee had returned and he had two friends with him. They had each grabbed one of my arms so that I could not break free.

"You think you're some kind of tough guy, don't you?" Pee Wee asked in his deep, gravelly voice. "Well, you don't look so bad now."

I glanced over to Brubaker. To my surprise, he stayed on the ground, apparently unwilling or unable to participate in the soon to be beating.

I knew there was no way I could take all three of these men, especially with my arms being held fast. The two men at either side of me were about my size, but Pee Wee was bigger than all three of us combined. I probably could have handled Pee Wee one on one, though perhaps not in my weakened condition after my fight with Brubaker. I had no chance under the current circumstances. I braced myself for a pretty bad ass kicking.

Then, from behind Pee Wee, I heard a familiar voice.

"Excuse me, sir?"

Pee Wee turned around quickly. He was so massive, I could still not see the other man, though I was pretty sure who it was.

"Get lost, old man," Pee Wee roared before turning back to me.

"Excuse me, sir?" the voice asked again.

This time, Pee Wee turned back with rage in his eyes.

"Okay, you asked for it!" he shouted.

He drew back his mammoth fist, but never landed his punch. Instead, I heard a *kiai* as either a kick or a punch struck Pee Wee. He screamed loudly and fell to the ground. As he hit the ground, he yelled, "Oh, my fucking balls, ohhhhh."

Now, I could see my rescuer. I had guessed right. Mr. Ito stood before me, a slight, almost playful smile on his face. It was only there for a split second before his expression hardened.

"Gentlemen," he said stoically, "I suggest you let my friend go."

For a moment, my captors just looked at each other. Then, the guy on my left yelled to his friend, "Get him, Seth!"

Seth let go of my arm and rushed toward Mr. Ito. As he did, I spun toward the guy holding my left arm and struck him between the eyes with the heel of my right hand. He released my arm and staggered back. Unwilling to fight without backup, he turned and ran off toward the woods.

I turned and saw Seth facing off with Mr. Ito, who just stood quietly waiting for the fool to attack him. Confused by the old man's refusal to move or fight, Seth threw a straight right hand at him.

With the speed and agility of a much younger man, Ito blocked the punch effortlessly and, in almost the same movement, punched him sharply in the stomach. Seth barely had time to grunt and lean forward before Ito spun to his right, put his arm around Seth's waist and threw him over his hip. Seth slammed into the ground. He writhed in pain, but had the sense to stay down, assuming of course he was even able to stand.

With all of the attackers either running away or on the ground in agony, I walked over to Mr. Ito.

"Thank you, Sensei," I said.

Ito shook his head immediately.

"We are not in class. Are we, Connor?"

"No, we are not," I admitted with a smile. "Thank you, Okada."

"Think nothing of it," he replied. "It was fun."

"How did you know where I was?" I asked. "I never told you where—"

I stopped myself, suddenly realizing the answer.

"Becky told you, didn't she?" I asked.

"Don't be angry with her," Ito said. "She was worried about you, and it would appear for good cause."

I wasn't angry with her. I knew she had been worried about me and instead of being angry, I found I was not only flattered, but also grateful.

"I can't argue with that," I conceded. "If you hadn't come along, it would have been pretty bad."

"No doubt," Ito said. "I would have been stuck doing the dojo paperwork for at least a month."

I was still laughing when the first Rockfield Police cruiser pulled up. Two officers got out of the car and quickly assessed the situation. They took a statement from Ito and myself. Pee Wee has still howling in pain and could barely breathe let alone give a statement. Seth was able to speak two or three words at a time.

"That guy... over there... beat up Paulie," he forced through his gasping for air. "I tried... to help..."

As he continued his drawn-out statement, Seth failed to mention the part about attacking me from behind.

Moments later, two more cruisers arrived. Out of one of the cars stepped Chief Taylor. He took a quick look around and walked over to me.

"Tell me exactly what happened," he commanded.

I told him everything, including Brubaker's confessions about Worthington and the planting of evidence. When I finished, Taylor looked at Ito who simply nodded.

"Officers," Taylor announced, "I want you to arrest these two men on the ground and Officer Brubaker as well."

The officers paused for a moment, surprised on being ordered to arrest one of their own.

"Did I stutter?" Taylor shouted.

"No, sir," the officers said in unison, before carrying out their instructions.

As Brubaker was taken into custody, I felt for the first time that I was finally in control of this case. I still didn't know who committed the murder, but I could prove it wasn't John Hardy.

CHAPTER TWENTY-TWO

Twenty minutes later, I was on my way home. Brubaker and his friends were en route to jail and Mr. Ito was following behind me in his Lincoln Continental. He had accepted my invitation to stop by my house for a beer. I owed him more than that, but a cold beer was all he would accept.

As I pulled into my driveway, I noticed the lights were on in my house. I wasn't worried because Becky's car was there. I parked alongside it and waited for Mr. Ito, who had chosen to park on the main street.

I smiled as he walked up my driveway.

"You sure are making me work for that beer," he said.

We were almost to the house when the front door flew open and Becky came running out. She came right to me and grabbed me in a full hug. I groaned a little when she squeezed me. The front of my shoulder was still tender from where Brubaker had kicked me.

"Are you okay?" she asked.

"I'm fine," I replied.

She released me and stared at me hard, allowing the front porch light to reveal my still bloody face. I had wiped off the blood with a handkerchief in my car, but it was still oozing out of my nose.

"You're fine, huh?" she challenged. "You're bleeding and you have a mouse under your eye."

I had seen the swelling under my left eye when I examined myself in my car's vanity mirror. By morning, it was going to be black and blue. I was probably going to be very sore, especially in my arms. Blocking those kicks had not been easy.

But, all things considered, I was far better off than Brubaker. In addition to the considerable damage to his elbow, I was certain he had broken his nose and his hand. Plus, his career as a police officer was likely over.

"It looks far worse than it is," I said, though not all convinced.

Becky scowled at me, apparently dissatisfied with my response.

"Besides," I continued, "you should see the other guy."

Becky laughed despite her efforts to remain angry with me. She quickly regained herself and looked over to Mr. Ito.

"Are you hurt?" she asked.

"My only ailment is a dry mouth," Ito said, with an absolutely straight face.

"What?" Becky asked in confusion.

"He means he has nothing that a cold beer wouldn't fix," I offered.

Becky gave him her best scowl and said something that sounded like "Hmmpf". Then, she returned her focus back to me.

"Well, let's go inside and get you cleaned up," she said. Looking back to Ito, she said, "And we'll get you that beer."

Once we were inside, I washed my hands and face. I quickly changed my shirt to one that was not covered in blood. Then, I got a couple of Heinekens for Ito and me. Becky already had a glass of wine poured for herself. I grabbed some tissues for my nose in case the bleeding resumed, and the three of us went out back to the patio. There were chairs for all three of us, and I lit a small fire in the pit to hold off the evening chill.

Once we were comfortable, Becky had me tell her the entire story of my encounter with Brubaker. I tried to downplay the times where he had kicked me, but the look on her face suggested I had failed. When I got to the part where I defeated Brubaker, I paused hoping for an "attaboy". Becky said nothing and had the same concerned look on her face, so I just continued.

She gasped when I revealed Brubaker's confession and the involvement of Worthington.

"Why that slimy worm!" she said in disgust. "That bum needs to go to jail!"

"He'll get his tomorrow morning at the preliminary hearing," I said. "I can't wait to see the look on his face."

Becky raised her glass in a mock toast.

"Tell her the rest," Mr. Ito prompted. He obviously wanted credit for his role in the fight. I guess I couldn't blame him. Taking down a monster like Pee Wee without even breaking a sweat was certainly an accomplishment.

"Okay," I conceded, "I will."

I explained to Becky how I was held fast by the two men while Pee Wee prepared to beat me senseless. Before I could continue, I was interrupted by Mr. Ito.

"So, I knew Connor was in trouble. I knew it was up to me," he said, trying to build suspense. "I approached the mammoth man knowing that soon he and I would be in a life-or-death struggle."

"Oh boy," I groaned quietly to myself.

Becky took no notice of me, as she was entranced by the thrilling tale being told. Although the basic facts of the story were true, Mr. Ito described the event in a grandiose, over-the-top way. I just sat back and let Mr. Ito have his moment. He had definitely earned it.

When Ito finished his riveting account, Becky glanced at me with a look that was part mischievous and part apprehensive.

Are you mad at me for telling him?" she asked.

I smiled. "How could I be?" I replied. "I was able to handle Brubaker, but Pee Wee and his two clowns were too much. I'm grateful for your help."

Ito smiled and stood. "Thank you for the beer, but it is getting late."

We walked him back through the house and to the front door. I thanked him again, but he just shrugged it off. Becky moved forward and hugged him warmly.

"Thank you for everything," she said, and then gave him a kiss on the cheek.

Mr. Ito seemed slightly embarrassed. I could not recall ever seeing him blush before now. He said nothing to Becky, but instead opened the door before turning to me.

"Would you like a little free advice?" he asked.

"Of course," I replied.

"Don't let this one get away," he said, pointing at Becky. "She's something special."

Without another word, he left, closing the door behind him.

Becky walked over to me and embraced me.

"Nothing to say to that advice, Mr. Big-Shot Lawyer?" she asked.

"Sounds like pretty good advice to me," I answered.

"Just pretty good?" Becky asked, her eyebrows arching with mock outrage.

I scooped her up in my arms and kissed her long and tenderly. I started walking with her toward the bedroom. I could feel the front of my shoulder complaining from the effort, but I ignored it.

I laid Becky onto the bed and sat beside her. I leaned down and kissed her again, this time with more fervor and passion. I pulled back slightly so I could make eye contact with her.

"*Damn* good advice," I said, before kissing her again. This time, I did not intend to stop.

I awoke the next morning bright and early. Becky was not there, but the smell of bacon and coffee in the air told me exactly where she was. *Damn*, I thought, *a night of passionate sex followed by a breakfast of coffee and bacon. Life doesn't get much better than that.*

Then, I moved, and my feeling of bliss was replaced by pain. I ached all over, particularly my arms, shoulders, and face. I forced myself to my feet and staggered into the bathroom. I looked in the mirror and saw an image that matched the way I felt. An ugly dark bruise ran underneath my eye to my nose and down to the edge of my lip. A worse bruise was on the front of my left shoulder and chest. My forearms were swollen and sore from blocking his kicks.

I knew that I was looking at two weeks of watching my face and chest turn all the colors of the rainbow.

My right elbow was tender as well. This was not so bad though. At least this injury was caused by me breaking Brubaker's nose. The others were from his kicks and hurt my pride as well as my body.

I took a quick shower and shaved. I dressed in a charcoal double-breasted suit with a bright yellow tie. Hardy's preliminary hearing was in two hours and I needed to look good. I already had a picture in the local paper of me in my black belt and gi. Now, photos at the hearing would show my bruises and swollen face. If I were careful, I could make sure only my right side was toward the cameras.

I laughed to myself as I looked into the mirror in my bedroom and turned sharply to my left. *I'm ready for my close-up, Mr. DeMille*, I thought.

I made my way down to the kitchen. Becky had bacon and coffee ready. As good as they were, they paled in comparison to how Becky looked. She was wearing one of my t-shirts and nothing else. The shirt went down maybe an inch below her behind. The rest of her legs glistened in the sunlight that came through the kitchen windows. They were mesmerizing. I could have spent the rest of the week eating bacon, drinking coffee, and looking at her legs.

"Did you hear me?"

Becky's voice brought me out of my trance.

"What?" I asked stupidly.

"I asked you if you were ready for the hearing today," Becky continued, "but you seem more interested in my legs."

"Damn straight," I said.

Her look told me that while she appreciated my enjoyment of her shapely legs, she wanted an answer to her question.

"Yes," I answered, "I'm ready. If the hearing takes place, then I expect the charges against Hardy will be dismissed today."

"What do you mean *if* the hearing happens?" she asked. "Why wouldn't it take place?"

"Usually, when the charge is really serious or if the victim of the crime is a child, the district attorney presents the case to a grand jury and avoids the need for the hearing." I said. "That's the usual procedure."

"What happens then, Connor?"

"We have a trial in county court in a few months," I answered.

Becky looked confused. She poured herself a cup of coffee, sat down in the chair next to me, and sipped it.

"So, what's the point of having the preliminary hearing?" she asked.

"Well, if the district attorney wants a defendant held in jail before an indictment, there has to be this hearing to make sure there is evidence to justify it."

Becky contemplated this for a moment. "Well, why wouldn't Worthington just have Judge Hardy indicted?" she asked. "He could avoid this hearing and keep him in jail."

It was a good question and one I had thought about myself. Worthington was not the sharpest legal mind, but even he would know this. Why give me a chance to see any of his evidence and cross examine witnesses?

"I don't know," I finally admitted. "Maybe he will. He has almost two hours before the hearing."

When Becky didn't say anything else, I resumed eating my breakfast. Becky drained her coffee and stood up.

"I have to go home and change," she said. "I'll meet you at the courthouse. I want to see this hearing."

"I expect half the town will be there to see it," I offered. "Get there early or you may not get a seat."

"Then, I better change back into my own clothes and get going," she said, heading for the hallway that led to the bedroom.

I looked back to my plate, but it was empty. I was just about to finish the last swallow of coffee when I heard Becky say, "I believe this is yours."

I looked up just as my t-shirt landed on my head. I pulled it off and saw Becky walking naked down the hall toward my bedroom. I watched intently until her lovely bare backside disappeared.

Life doesn't get much better than that, I thought.

CHAPTER TWENTY-THREE

"**D**id you get the license plate of the truck that ran over your face?" was the question that greeted me as I walked through the door into my law office.

"Good morning to you too, Casey," I answered sarcastically, as I walked past her and into my inner office.

Now settled in my chair, looking through some documents, Casey appeared again, holding two mugs of coffee. Though I had already consumed two cups at home, I decided that I could still use a third.

Casey sat down in one the client chairs and sipped her coffee.

"Are you going to tell me what happened?" she asked.

I could see that despite the tone of her voice, there was genuine concern in her eyes. I also knew the bruise on my face looked kind of gruesome. So, I explained about the fight from the night before.

"We have an ice pack upstairs if you need it," she offered.

"No, thank you," I said. "I have to get ready for the hearing. Besides, it makes me look tough."

"If you say so, Connor," Casey snickered. "Maybe we should take a photo of you."

"Now, why would I want to do that?"

Can't you just see it?" she asked. "A huge billboard with that picture."

She held out her hands as if she were placing words on this imagined billboard.

Then, through her growing laughter, she said, "Connor Phelan—He fights for his clients."

"All right," I said, "I'm never going to live down that picture of me in court wearing my gi and belt, am I?"

"No way," she said with a bright smile.

She took another sip of coffee before mercifully changing the subject. "By the way, Miss Bollenbacher called at 8:58 am and demanded an update on the Hardy case. She's called twice since then."

"She certainly is persistent," I answered.

"Old Iron Girdle is a genuine pain in the ass who won't take no for an answer," she said, shaking her head in defiance. "I'd appreciate it if you'd return her call. She must have called twenty times in the last two days demanding an update."

"She's certainly determined," I replied.

"What she is, is a—"

I held up my hand to cut her off.

"I get the picture. I'll call her before I leave for court."

"Thank God," Casey retorted, as she stood up and walked through the door. "That woman is driving me absolutely..."

Her mumbling faded as she got further away. Though I could still hear her talking, I could no longer make out the words.

I took a strong pull from the coffee and braced myself as I called Ethel "Old Iron Girdle" Bollenbacher.

"Good morning, Mr. Phelan," she answered.

I always hated it when people did that. I knew most people had caller ID now, but I guess I missed the old days when you didn't know who was calling until you actually answered the phone.

"Good morning," I replied, as cheerily as I could muster. "I'm just returning your calls."

"Mr. Phelan," she said defiantly, "I retained your services and I expect regular updates. Thus far, I have struggled to even get you on the phone."

"As I have told you before, ma'am," I interjected, "Judge Hardy is my client. I realize that you paid for the initial retainer. However, what I can disclose to you is limited."

"When I pay for something," she demanded, "I expect to get what I paid for."

Her tone was starting to annoy me. Yet, I forced myself to remain polite. I could hear my mother speaking to me as a child reminding me of the importance of showing respect to my elders. It was a lesson I had learned well and had sometimes learned the hard way.

"Miss Bollenbacher, as I have said, it is limited what I can tell you in this—"

"I have heard this song before, young man," she interrupted.

"I know that you have, ma'am," I pressed. "But I—"

"Mr. Phelan," she interjected in a tone louder than talking, but not quite to the level of shouting. "I want to know right now what evidence they have against John Hardy." I looked down at my watch. I really didn't have time for a long conversation. I decided that I would give her a brief outline of the evidence. I didn't want to, but I had to give her something so she would stop calling and being a general pest.

"Okay, ma'am, I only have a few minutes before I have to leave for court, but since I know you care about the judge, I'll give you a brief outline. Will that suffice?"

The line went quiet as she considered my words.

"It will do," she finally replied, before adding, "for now."

"The main evidence against him is DNA," I said.

"How did they get that?" she pressed.

"Look," I said firmly, "if you want me to discuss the evidence, you need to let me do so. I do not have time for a question-and-answer session,"

"Fine," she said flatly. "Please proceed."

"They have Hardy's DNA that they obtained from hair found on the victim's body," I continued.

"What?" she said sharply. "But, how in the hell did they find—"

"Miss Bollenbacher," I interrupted forcefully.

"Sorry," she said curtly.

"I don't have time for all the details," I continued, "but the main part of the prosecution's case is the DNA evidence. I feel quite confident that I can deal with that."

"Is that it?" she asked, almost surprised. That's their entire case?"

"It's all they have to directly connect John Hardy," I said. "Everything else is circumstantial."

"Such as?" she asked.

"Look, I really do not have time—"

"Young man," Bollenbacher snapped, "as a paying client I have the right to know the evidence."

"You are not the client," I insisted. "My client is John Hardy."

"Who do you think asked me to hire you?" Bollenbacher roared. "Now, I want to know what circumstantial evidence they have against him."

I was beyond frustrated. This woman was not going to take no for an answer. I could just hang up, but she would probably come straight to the office. I would be gone by the time she got here, but that would leave Casey to deal with her. Though Casey would handle it, I would get an earful when I returned.

"Miss Bollenbacher, listen to me very carefully," I said slowly. "I will discuss one other piece of evidence with you now, and then I am hanging up and leaving for court. You are welcome to attend the hearing this morning. It is open to the public."

"Fine," she replied curtly, "but we will discuss this in further detail in the future."

How does John Hardy put up with this person? I thought.

"There is a partial video of the murder," I said. "It does not reveal the identity of the murderer, but it shows that Gilbert Russell was driven to the site of his hanging in an old pickup truck."

"Does it reveal the license plate?" Bollenbacher asked.

"No, it does not," I said in exasperation. "I'm leaving for court now."

She tried to speak again, but I cut her off.

"Goodbye," I said and hung up the phone.

I sat back in my chair, closed my eyes, and let out a breath in a loud sigh. My eyes were still closed two minutes later when the intercom buzzed again. I pressed the button hard.

"I'm not talking to Ethel Bollenbacher again," I said loudly.

"I don't blame you," Casey said over the intercom. "But the call is from Mrs. Edwards."

"Oh," I said almost foolishly, as I picked up the receiver and pressed line one. "Hello?"

"Good morning, Connor," Mrs. Edwards said in her kind voice. "I just wanted to thank you for taking care of those hoodlums and hooligans."

I smiled when I heard her words.

"My pleasure, ma'am," I said. "I take it they have not been back?"

"Oh no," she said. "The morning after your fight, Chief Taylor came over with two of his officers. They went into the old shed and looked around. You'll never guess what they found."

I waited for her to say something, but she didn't. She really wanted me to guess. I never liked guessing games.

"I don't know," I said. "What did they find?"

"They found three or four bags of marijuana," she announced. "Can you believe it? Marijuana on my property. Why, it's scandalous!"

I bit my lower lip to keep from laughing.

"That explains why they kept coming on your property," I said.

"It sure does," she added. "Chief Taylor told me that since I never use the old shed, those hoodlums decided it would be a good place to store their... well... stuff."

I thought that if I bit any harder on my lower lip, it would bleed. Still, it now made sense. I hadn't been sure why those punks had been bothering her. Now, I knew.

"What will people think when they find out that there was marijuana in my shed?" she asked. Her voice showed genuine concern. "I would never be involved with such things."

Mrs. Edwards was a very proud woman. She had taught school for decades and had been the president of her church council and a highly respected citizen. In fact, I doubt there was anyone in Rockfield more universally loved. She actually thought that people would think she had somehow been involved either in using or selling drugs. It was laughable, but I knew she was being serious. She thought she would be branded a hoodlum and hooligan.

I quickly thought of a way to alleviate her fear and give her peace of mind.

"I can tell you exactly what they will think," I offered.

"What?"

"They will say that Mrs. Harriet Edwards fought back against drug dealers and will not tolerate such things on her land."

"You think so?" she asked hesitantly, her voice sounding a little more reassured.

"Of course," I said confidently. "You never would have tolerated that in your classroom. Right?"

"Absolutely not," she replied sharply, her teacher's voice coming back to her.

"Then you wouldn't tolerate it at your home either," I concluded.

I didn't actually think those punks were drug dealers. They might have been. More likely they just bought and sold a few bags of grass for their own use and maybe for a few friends. Since all three were deadbeats who still lived with their parents, they just needed a place to hide it.

Whatever their motivation, it was more important to me to make sure that Mrs. Edwards was safe and that her dignity was unharmed.

After a brief silence, she said, "Thank you for everything, Connor."

"My pleasure, ma'am."

"Are you going to be in your office today?" she asked.

"Well, I have a hearing shortly, but I should be here after lunch," I answered. "Are you planning to visit?"

"Would that be all right?"

"Absolutely, Mrs. Edwards," I replied. "You are always welcome."

"Very well," she said. "I will be there after lunch and I am bringing your fee."

"The cookies?" I asked hopefully.

"Of course," she said. "A deal is a deal."

"Yes, ma'am," I said. "See you then."

I ended the phone call. I gathered up the documents on my desk and placed them back into the case folder before putting the whole thing into my trial bag. I picked up the bag and headed for the exit.

As I passed Casey, I said, "If Dom calls, please ask him to meet me at the courthouse. Okay?

"No problem," Casey answered. "I'll hold down the fort."

Just before I left, I heard Casey speak again.

"Good luck, Connor."

CHAPTER TWENTY-FOUR

W hen I parked in the courthouse lot, I noticed four news trucks from various Albany television stations. Men and women stood by large cameras on tripods waiting to go live with their updates.

I entered the building and made my way toward the very same metal detector I went through just days before. This time, I was properly dressed for court. The court officer recognized me and waved me in.

Standing in the lobby were even more people with much smaller portable news cameras. They were perfectly stationed to film people going in and out of the main courtroom. They could not go inside as cameras are banned in New York courts except under rare circumstances.

Too bad, I thought, *the public at large should see what an asshole Judge Marino is.*

I pushed open the courtroom door and walked inside. The gallery was nearly filled with spectators. I saw Becky sitting in the third row behind the defense table. She flashed her beautiful smile when she saw me.

In the assembled crowd, I also saw Ethel Bollenbacher,

Chief Taylor, Sheriff Sanders, and Mr. and Mrs. Lawson, the parents of the poor girl Gilbert Russell had murdered.

Seated in the two rows in front of Becky, but behind both prosecution and defense tables, was the rest of the media. The reporters from the local papers and radio stations were followed by the reporters from Albany. Since they could not record audio of the proceedings without permission of the judge, they had pads and pencils at the ready.

I walked down the middle aisle and opened the gate leading to the attorneys' tables and the judge's bench. The court stenographer was already in her seat, so I knew Judge Marino intended to start shortly.

District Attorney Worthington and a young assistant district attorney, whose name I did not know, were seated at the prosecution table reviewing their file. Neither looked up as I made my way to my seat.

I opened my trial bag and took out my case folder. I set it on the table, but did not open it. I then took a white legal pad and two pens out of the bag and placed them directly in front of me.

I had just finished testing my pens to see if they worked when I heard a door behind the judge's bench open. I looked up, expecting to see Judge Marino. However, his door was closed. It was the door that connected to the clerk's office that had opened. A large sheriff's deputy stood there holding the door open. A moment later, Judge Hardy walked through.

Although he was not in the jail, he was still considered to be within the custody of the sheriff. As such, the deputies had gone to his home and driven him to the courthouse. Hardy still had his ankle monitor on him, but he was also handcuffed. This was not a surprise. Anytime a prisoner was transported in a sheriff's department vehicle, he or she had to be cuffed.

Unlike most other prisoners, Hardy was not wearing a jail jumpsuit. He was dressed in a navy-blue suit with an extremely loud red tie. His Italian designer shoes were polished to a high shine.

Hardy was escorted to the defense table. The handcuffs were removed and he sat next to me.

"Good morning," he said cheerfully.

"You're certainly in a good mood," I noted.

"That's called confidence, my boy," he responded.

He then turned in his chair to gaze at the people gathered for the hearing. He waved to several people cordially.

I tapped him discreetly on his arm. He turned back to me.

"Yes?"

"This is not a campaign rally, John," I chided. "You're charged with murder."

"I know that, Connor," he said softly, "but I'm not giving Worthington the satisfaction of seeing me sweat or worry."

I understood his logic and cast a quick glance over to Worthington. He had looked up and was angrily glaring at Hardy. I guess John's high spirits were bothering him.

Fine by me, I thought. *I'll take any advantage I can get.*

"You seem troubled, Connor," Hardy said. "Everything okay?"

"Something's not right," I said.

"What is it?" Hardy asked, the first sign of concern crossing his face,

"I can't understand why this hearing is even taking place," I said. "If I were prosecuting, I would have just presented the case to the grand jury and avoided this entire hearing."

Hardy burst out laughing when he heard my words. I certainly did not expect that.

"He can't indict me," Hardy pronounced.

"Oh really?" I asked sarcastically.

"Would you like to know why?" Hardy asked with a touch of flair in his voice.

"By all means, John."

"He can't have me indicted because the grand jury is not in session," he said.

I just looked at him dumbfounded.

"John, what are you talking about?" I asked. "The grand jury runs almost constantly."

"Almost," he said with a wide smile, "but not quite."

I turned my chair so I was facing Hardy and looked him directly in the eyes.

"All right John, out with it,"

"As you know, the grand jury is impaneled by the county court judge," Hardy noted.

"Yes, I know this, John," but what are you getting at? Cut to the chase."

"Oh, very well," Hardy said, almost a little disappointed. "The grand jury I constituted is currently in recess. So, they cannot convene."

"That won't matter," I said. "The district attorney has the right to request the grand jury be reconvened."

"Yes, that's right," Hardy agreed. "But, under the criminal procedure law, it is the court that must rule on that request. I am not on the bench, so I cannot rule on his request, now, can I?"

"You're not the only judge that can do that," I said. "Any New York Supreme Court judge can do that."

Hardy just smiled, winked, and crossed his arms in satisfaction. I pondered the matter for a moment and realized what had happened. There was only one Supreme Court judge with chambers in the county, Francis O'Connor.

"Where's Judge O'Connor?" I asked.

"Well, he left shortly after ordering my release on a two-week fishing trip," he replied with a sly smile on his face.

"Let me guess," I offered. "He wouldn't by chance be staying at your fishing cabin up in the Adirondacks?"

John didn't say anything. He just winked again and smiled broadly.

I had to admit. John had set things up nicely. Without Judge O'Connor or himself available, it would take at least a week to get another Supreme Court Judge to reconvene the grand jury. By then, the statutory time period would have expired and Hardy would have to be released.

Worthington was left with the choice of doing the hearing and allowing his evidence to be challenged or refusing to do the hearing. If he refused, Hardy would be ordered released even from home confinement and Worthington would have to explain why he allowed someone charged with murder to be set free. That would make Worthington look weak in the eyes of the public. His ego couldn't stand that.

"You know you could have told me all this before now?"

"Better you didn't know, my boy," Hardy offered. "It's called plausible deniability."

Part of me found Hardy's antics amusing, while another part of me wanted to kick him squarely in the pants. I decided to let it go and focus on the upcoming hearing.

About a minute later, Dom came up to the table and took the last seat.

"Connor, we have to talk," he said through heavy breathing. "We have a problem."

"What is it?" I asked.

At that moment, the voice of the court bailiff shouted out.

"All rise. The Rockfield City Court is now in session. The Honorable Marcus Marino presiding."

Everyone in the court stood. I desperately wanted to know what problem Dom was talking about, but I couldn't ask him now.

Judge Marino strode to his chair and sat down.

"Please be seated," he said without looking up from the papers before him.

"This is the case of the People of the State of New York versus John J. Hardy," he announced. "We are here for the required preliminary hearing. Are the People ready to proceed?"

Worthington stood. "Yes, Your Honor," he crowed in his whiny voice.

Marino looked toward me. "Is the defense ready?"

I stood to address the court. "Yes, judge. However—"

"Mr. Phelan," the judge interrupted, "why is there always a but or a however?"

"I can't answer that, judge," I replied, keeping my voice as respectful as possible. "May counsel approach the bench please?"

Marino did not reply verbally. Instead, he just signaled with both hands for us to come forward.

Worthington and I walked up to the bench. Marino turned off his microphone and leaned forward in his chair.

"Make it quick, Mr. Phelan," he grumbled.

"Your Honor, the defense has a witness we wish to call today."

"What's that to me, counsel?" the judge asked sourly.

"Our witness is currently in the county jail," I said. "I need an order from you to transport him here."

"Really?" the judge said almost sarcastically, "and who is that?"

"Paul Brubaker," I replied.

"Officer Brubaker?" the judge asked, a look of astonishment on his face. "Why is he in jail?"

Since Marino didn't know about the arrest, that told me that Brubaker had not been formally arraigned. He had been arrested somewhat late the previous night. Maybe he was being arraigned later today.

"Your honor," I continued, "Officer Brubaker was arrested last night for assault and for suspicion of tampering with evidence."

"I can assure the Court," Worthington interjected, "that Officer Brubaker was not charged with any such thing."

"I was there when he was arrested, judge," I insisted.

Marino held up both hands. "Enough, counselors. Let's take this to my chambers. Go back to your tables."

As Worthington and I returned to our seats, Judge Marino addressed the entire courtroom.

"We are going to take a brief recess so that I may handle some preliminary matters in my chambers.," he announced. "The defendant will remain where he is and I expect to resume the bench in no more than fifteen minutes."

The judge stood and headed for the door to his chambers. The bailiff quickly called for the people to stand. Maybe half were able to get to their feet before the door slammed behind the judge.

As soon as he left, I turned to Dom.

"What's going on, boss?"

"Connor, I just found out that Brubaker was released."

"What?" I answered in a voice so loud it caused several people to look my way. I made sure to lower my voice when I spoke again.

"What do you mean he was released?"

Dom stepped closer to me so others wouldn't hear.

"I got a call about two hours ago from Chief Taylor. They charged Brubaker with assault, tampering with evidence, and official misconduct."

"Then why was he released?" I demanded.

"According to Jim, he went home while they were writing

up the charges. When he came in this morning, he found out that Brubaker was gone. His officers let Brubaker make his phone call. Take a guess who he called."

"Worthington," I answered scornfully.

"Give the man a cigar," Dom said sarcastically. "As district attorney, he ordered Brubaker released and announced that his office was declining to prosecute all of the charges."

"Son of a bitch," I said in frustration. "What time was he released?"

"Just before midnight," Dom answered. "I went by his house as soon as I heard from Taylor. He wasn't there. So, I let myself in. Most of his clothes were gone. Looked like he packed in a hurry."

"I bet," I said. "He could be almost anywhere. He's had a huge head start."

"I know exactly where he is," Dom said.

"I'm almost afraid to ask," I said apprehensively. "Where is he?"

"He's on an airplane to Chicago,"

I couldn't believe my ears. Worthington had managed to get all of the charges dismissed and Brubaker released. Then, to top it all off, he arranged for him to take an immediate flight to Chicago. From a city of that size, Brubaker could disappear to nearly anywhere in the world.

Without another word, I started walking to the judge's chambers.

CHAPTER TWENTY-FIVE

When I walked into the judge's chambers, both Worthington and Marino were already seated. Marino had a scowl etched into his face.

"You certainly took long enough, Mr. Phelan," he said acerbically. "Can we get on with this please?"

"Yes, judge," I answered, as I took a seat.

"Now," the judge continued, "will somebody tell me about Officer Brubaker?"

"Please allow me, your honor," Worthington offered in his snooty nasal voice.

Wanting to hear what he would say, I did not object.

"Go ahead, Mr., Worthington," the judge replied.

"Thank you, your honor," the district attorney began. "Last night, the Rockfield Police Department took Officer Brubaker into custody after a fight with Mr. Phelan."

Judge Marino looked over at me.

"Is that true, Mr. Phelan?" he asked.

"Partially, judge," I conceded, pointing at the bruise on my face.

The judge raised his eyebrows, looked back at Worthington, and said, "Continue."

With a smug look, Worthington resumed his story.

"After some kind of confrontation, Mr. Phelan and Officer Brubaker engaged in fisticuffs."

I wondered to myself if there was anyone else in a hundred-mile radius who still used the word *fisticuffs*.

"As a result," Worthington continued, "Mr. Brubaker suffered significant injuries to his elbow and hand."

Marino glanced over to me for confirmation.

"He means I won the fight," I offered.

Marino frowned. "I did *not* need a translation counselor."

"Sorry, judge."

"I am concerned, however," the judge continued, "that you were in a fight with a witness in this case."

"I went to interview him, judge," I responded. "In the course of that interview, he attacked me. I simply defended myself."

"Mr. Brubaker says otherwise, judge," Worthington chimed in. "He says Mr. Phelan attacked him and tried to force him to recant his intended testimony."

"That's a lie, Worthington," I challenged.

"That's enough, gentlemen," the judge ordered.

When the room was quiet, Marino pointed at the district attorney. "Continue, Mr. Worthington," he droned.

"Anyway," Worthington said, his annoyance apparent, "the police took Officer Brubaker into custody based on some outrageous claims by Mr. Phelan. I personally reviewed the charges and found them lacking. So, I dismissed them and had the poor man released."

"And sent to Chicago," I challenged.

"I have no idea what you are talking about, counselor."

"The hell you don't," I shouted, jumping to my feet. "You

took care of the charges and put Brubaker on a plane to Chicago to cover up what you did."

"That's an outrageous lie," Worthington shouted back, though he remained in his seat.

"Calm down, Mr. Phelan," the judge admonished.

"Judge, this man is trying to frame my client for his own—"

"How dare you!" Worthington screamed, finally coming to his feet.

Marino himself stood up; his face flushed with anger.

"Both of you sit down and shut up!" the judge roared. "I will have no more of this!"

Worthington and I glared at each other intently. After a few seconds, Worthington broke eye contact with me and abruptly sat down. I waited another second and then sat.

Marino waited for a few seconds before he sat down. Then, he looked at me.

"Is Mr. Brubaker in the county jail or is he in Chicago, Mr. Phelan?"

"To the best of my knowledge, he is currently on a plane bound for Chicago," I replied.

"In that case, counselor, why are you asking me for an order to produce him from the county jail?"

"When I made the request, I believed he was in the jail," I explained. "En route to your chambers, I was advised by my investigator that Brubaker had been released and put on a plane to Chicago."

Worthington started to speak, but Marino waved him off.

"If the witness is on an airplane, there's no need for an order from me and it is fair to say that he will not be testifying at this hearing," the judge said. "Both of you return to the courtroom. I will be out to conduct this hearing in ten minutes."

I got up and walked out into the hallway. I walked halfway down the corridor, stopped, and waited for Worthington. He came along about thirty seconds later. As soon as I saw him, I went right at him.

He stopped suddenly when he saw me, his eyes wide with fear. I got so close to him, I could almost have worn his shirt.

"You pathetic son of a bitch," I growled. "You may have gotten rid of Brubaker, but we both know you tried to frame John Hardy."

"I have no idea what you are talking about, counselor," he sniveled. "I am just prosecuting this case."

Although I wanted to drop him on his snide behind, I knew this would accomplish nothing. He would just have me arrested. So, I stepped back and let him pass.

He was only a few steps ahead of me when he stopped and turned back to me.

"Besides, even if it were true, you can't prove it."

Then, with a smug and arrogant smile, he turned and walked away from me.

I was blazing mad and had very little time before the hearing resumed. I knew I had to regain my composure. So, I went to the men's room to splash some cold water on my face. As I wiped off the water, I glanced in the mirror above the sink. My bruise still looked ugly. I made a promise to myself that somehow Worthington would pay for his treachery. First and foremost, however, I was going to win this preliminary hearing today come hell or high water. I took a deep breath and headed for the courtroom.

When I sat down at the defense table, both Dom and Hardy leaned toward me.

"Everything all right?" Dom asked.

"No," I said truthfully, "but we're not going to let that stop us, are we?"

Judge Marino resumed the bench at precisely the ten-minute mark. He did not even instruct the assembled crowd to sit after his entrance.

"Mr. Worthington, call your first witness, please," the judge ordered. "We have already wasted a great deal of time and I want to move this matter along."

Worthington stood. "The People call Dr. Randy Young to the stand."

Dr. Young stood and began walking toward the witness chair. Once he was sworn in as a witness, Worthington went to the podium with a small packet of white papers. He had obviously written out all of the questions he planned to ask.

"Dr. Young, what is your position with Linton County?" Worthington asked, without ever looking up from his papers.

"I am the County Coroner, sir."

Worthington slid his finger slightly down the page.

"Dr. Young, did there come a time when you conducted an autopsy on Russell Gilbert?"

"Yes, counselor, I did."

Worthington again slid his finger down the page before his next question.

Holy shit, I thought. *He has to read off a prepared text.* I was quietly laughing to myself when I realized something. *What if he has to go off his planned script?*

"What were the results of—"

"Excuse me, your honor," I said, rising to my feet, "but in the interest of moving this matter along, the defense will stipulate to the contents of the good doctor's autopsy report."

"Very well," the judge replied. "The court will accept the doctor's report into evidence for this hearing. May I have a copy please?"

Worthington seemed momentarily confused. Submitting the report was not supposed to happen yet. He ran his finger down the page as quickly as he could, trying to find the proper place.

"Mr. Worthington?" the judge inquired. "The report?"

"Uh, yes judge," Worthington answered. Then, he stopped sliding his finger. He apparently had found his place.

"Your Honor," he announced, "I offer the autopsy report into evidence."

The judge looked at him like he had three heads.

"The court has already accepted the document into evidence, counselor," the judge said testily. "I just want the document presented."

Worthington began scanning his script again hopelessly looking for an answer.

"Your Honor," I said. "If I may approach the bench, the defense has a copy of the autopsy report."

"Fine, fine," Marino grunted. "Can we please move this along?"

"Of course, judge," I said sweetly. I then brought the autopsy report to the bench and handed it to the judge.

I was not even back to my table when the judge began prompting the confused district attorney.

"Any more questions?" he asked.

"Uh, yes judge," Worthington said. He looked down to his script and just picked up where he left off.

"Doctor, can you tell the court your professional opinion as to cause of death?"

"Objection, your honor," I said. I didn't have to stand as I hadn't even had a chance to sit yet.

"Mr. Worthington," the judge admonished angrily, "the autopsy report is in evidence. It establishes the cause of death and that Gilbert Russell was the victim of homicide."

Worthington looked like a deer in the headlights. He had rarely handled court proceedings and was out of his element. He was a paper lawyer and an administrator, not to mention an asshole.

He glanced over to his associate for help. She mouthed the words, *No further questions.*

Worthington looked back to the judge and parroted, "No further questions." As he walked back to his desk, red-faced with embarrassment, the judge asked me if I wished to question the witness.

I considered it. It was a good opportunity to get some additional information. However, I felt keeping the pressure on Worthington was a better plan.

"No questions, judge," I said.

Marino glared at me for a moment before moving his gaze back to Worthington.

"Your next witness?"

Worthington's assistant handed him another folder. The district attorney opened it and took out act two of his script.

"The People call Cameron Sears to the stand."

A woman with dark hair and glasses stood and began walking toward the witness chair. I recognized her name immediately. She was the lab technician who compared the hair samples planted by Brubaker and Hardy's DNA.

"Excuse me, judge," I said. "May I be heard?"

"Is it really necessary, counsel?" Marino said.

"It would help move things along, judge," I offered helpfully.

"Very well," he conceded. "What is it?"

"This witness is being offered to testify that she compared the DNA sample of the defendant to DNA taken from hairs *allegedly* found on the victim's body," I said. "We will concede all of that."

"You will?" Judge Marino and DA Worthington said at the same time.

"Yes," I replied. "However, we do not concede that the hairs were actually found on the body. It is our contention that they were planted there."

"That's not true," Worthington roared. "Mr. Phelan is trying to—"

"What I am trying to do," I interrupted, "is hold the People to their proof. They have to prove that the hair was actually found on Gilbert Russell's body."

"Judge," Worthington whined, "I would like to present my own case in my own way."

"We've already seen what a disaster that was," I noted.

"I object to that," Worthington shouted.

The judge held up his hands again. "Enough! Not another word!" he shouted. He waited to make sure his court was quiet before continuing.

"Mr. Worthington, is the defense correct about what your witness will say?"

"Well... yes, judge." he admitted.

"Then, the court accepts the stipulation," Marino said. "The only issue left is to establish who found the hair on the body. Mr. Worthington?"

Worthington looked worried. He turned to his associate who immediately handed him another folder. He opened it and scanned the contents.

"Your Honor, the People offer these reports from Officer Paul Brubaker which clearly establish that he was the one who—"

"Objection, your honor," I called out. "I have the right to cross examine Brubaker. His reports cannot be entered into evidence without him testifying to their authenticity."

"That's true, Mr. Worthington," the judge agreed.

"But I can't call Officer Brubaker," Worthington protested. "He's on his way to Chicago."

"Then you shouldn't have put him on a plane," I interjected.

Worthington whirled around to me, rage in his eyes. He opened his mouth to speak, but never got a chance.

"Mr. Worthington?" the judge yelled out. "I'm up here."

The district attorney turned back around and faced the judge.

"Yes, judge?"

"I agree with Mr. Phelan. Your request to enter the documents is denied."

"But, Judge, I really think—"

"What you *think* is of no consequence to this court," the judge replied.

I kept quiet, but inside I was laughing to beat all hell.

"Do you have any more witnesses?" the judge demanded.

Worthington once again looked to his assistant for help. She simply shook her head.

"No, your honor, we have no more further witnesses."

I stood up knowing I had the hearing won. For the prosecution to win, they had to show that the defendant committed a felony in the State of New York. They had shown that a felony was committed; the murder of Gilbert Russell. They had offered no evidence; however, to show that John Hardy committed that felony.

"Your honor," I said confidently, "at this time, I move for   "

"Save your breath, Mr. Phelan," the judge chided. "I can take it from here. I find that the prosecution has not met their burden of proof. The felony complaint against John J. Hardy is dismissed. We are adjourned."

He banged his gavel, stood up and headed for the door to his chambers. The court officer quickly asked everyone to stand.

Once the judge was through the door, John Hardy extended his hand to me.

"Great job, Connor," he said happily.

The case was not finished. Worthington could look to

reinstate the charges. Within days, a Supreme Court Judge from outside the county would reinstate the grand jury. If Brubaker returned to Linton County, an indictment could be obtained quickly.

The fight was not over just yet.

CHAPTER TWENTY-SIX

The moment that the judge closed the door behind him, the courtroom became busy with excitement. Some reporters were scurrying to get outside so they could file their reports or perhaps go live from the courthouse with late breaking news. Others were calling out asking for comments from Worthington, Hardy, or myself. I held Hardy at the defense table. I did not want him talking to the media. Moments later, Worthington and his associate made their way down the aisle toward the exit. Reporters swirled around hoping for a statement.

I heard Worthington's associate say, "No comment," at least three times.

The only time Worthington spoke, he said something about the murderer of Gilbert Russell being brought to justice.

I felt a tug on my arm. I looked and saw Becky. She had been able to get through, only after the reporters started following Worthington.

"Not too shabby," she offered with a brilliant smile.

In truth, all I had really done was let Worthington make an ass of himself. It wasn't particularly difficult. But, earned or not,

I wasn't about to turn down the chance to see Becky smile. It was something so uplifting to behold. If you saw it, you understood. If not, you truly missed something.

As much as I wanted to enjoy that smile, I knew that as soon as Worthington got in his car and pulled away, the reporters would be back looking for me. Worse, I could see Ethel Bollenbacher making her way towards us through the crowd. I had no desire for another verbal sparring session with her.

"Dom, can you convince the police to let us use one of the back exits? I really don't want to deal with the crowd right now."

"No problem," Dom promised, and headed over to one of the court officers.

He spoke with him for a moment and then waved us over.

"We're going through the same door Hardy came in," he announced. "They have to remove his ankle monitor before he can leave."

I quickly jammed everything into my trial bag, closed it, and moved for the door. We got through before the media or Bollenbacher could make contact.

Beyond was a long corridor that led into the police station. We passed some holding cells on our left and reached a metal door. The officer pulled out some keys and opened it. Two sheriff's deputies were waiting on the other side. They invited us in.

Inside was the police station itself. We were brought to a small conference room where the deputies removed Hardy's ankle monitor and had him sign a few papers. Then, we were free to go.

I gave my car keys to Becky, so she could pull my car around front. The reporters did not know her and would leave her alone. If Dom or I went for our cars, we would be surrounded in seconds.

A few minutes later, Becky was back and handed me the keys.

"I'll take John home and meet you at headquarters," I said.

"Oh, no," Hardy protested. "I've been stuck inside my home for days. That's the last place I want to be."

"All right," I agreed. "I'll bring you to headquarters. We can talk about the next step in your case."

"Fine," Hardy said. "But, can we stop at Fast Freddy's first? I'm dying for a hot dog."

Fast Freddy's Wiener Shop was a Rockfield mainstay. They were famous for hotdogs with homemade hot sauce, onions, and mustard. There were none quite like it.

"You take the judge to the office," Dom said. "I'll get Becky to her car and pick up some dogs on the way. Good enough?'

"Good enough," Hardy agreed.

Hardy and I went outside. My car was waiting there. Thankfully, no reporters were there either. They must have been on the other side of the building at the court entrance. We climbed into my Cherokee and took off.

Almost thirty minutes later, Dom and Becky entered my office with the smell of hot sauce coming from several bags they carried. Between the four of us and Casey, we devoured more than a dozen dogs. It wasn't gourmet, but it was delicious.

After finishing his fourth and final dog, Hardy wiped his mouth with a napkin and sat back in his chair.

"So, my boy, what's next?"

"Well," I replied, "that's kind of up to Worthington."

"How do you figure?" Dom asked.

"With the charges dismissed, it's up to Worthington to decide if he wants to present the case to a grand jury," I offered. "If he does and gets an indictment, then we start over in either county court or supreme court."

"I'm not going to reconvene them," Hardy announced.

"It doesn't matter," I countered. "If you refuse, they'll get another judge to do it in a week or so. Besides, you can't keep Judge O'Connor in the Adirondacks forever."

"You've obviously never seen him fish," Hardy replied.

"Connor, do you really think Brubaker will come back for the grand jury?" Casey asked.

As usual, Casey's instincts were right on the nose. This was the big question. Without Brubaker, there was no case against Hardy.

"I don't know if Worthington can risk that," Becky answered for me, causing Dom, Hardy, and Casey to snap their heads toward her in stunned surprise.

Becky didn't often say much around them about cases, but I knew that she was a voracious reader of both true crime and fictional detective stories. She probably had over a thousand books in her collection. So, although she had little or no direct experience in criminal law, she often had outstanding insight from her reading.

Seeing the shocked look on their faces, Becky explained her statement.

"Brubaker planted the hair on the body on instructions from Worthington, right?"

I nodded.

"Well, if he brings him back, he has to worry about Brubaker dropping a dime on him." Becky said with a satisfied smile.

I smiled. Few people other than Sam Spade or Mike Hammer still used *dropping a dime* anymore. Her point was well taken though.

"Dropping a dime?" Casey asked. She was too young to have heard of the expression.

"It would be a huge risk bringing him back," I agreed, ignoring Casey's question. "Chief Taylor has no intention of letting him stay on with the Rockfield Police. But, if he made a deal for immunity in return for testifying against Worthington, he could stay out of jail and possibly pick up with another department somewhere."

It was quiet as I considered the problem further.

"On the other hand," I offered, "if Worthington brought him back, he could give him immunity himself as district attorney and hire him as his chief investigator. Then, Brubaker avoids jail and gets a promotion."

"He'll do the latter," Hardy interjected. "Worthington is a control freak. The idea of Brubaker being out there and having the ability to take him down at any time would be too much for Worthington to handle. He'll bring him back for sure."

It got quiet as the implications of Hardy's words hit home.

"Well, then," I said, breaking the silence, "we need to solve this murder and fast."

Nobody had anything else to offer.

A few minutes later, Dom and Becky left. Becky had to get ready for work and Dom wanted to see if he could arrange for Brubaker to be found in Chicago. It was a longshot, but worth a try.

I offered to drive John Hardy home, but he still was not interested. I knew he did not want to be alone in his big house again, so I let him stay in the office. We talked about his case for a while, though much more time was spent listening to John talk about anything and everything.

Casey was smart enough after just a few minutes of this to announce that she had to go back to her desk and get some work done. As she left, she looked at me and winked. It was her way of saying, *better you than me.*

I tried picking up some papers on my desk to hint to John that I too had work to do. He failed to notice and started another story. Ten minutes later, he had just finished his tall tale when there was a knock at my door.

I looked up and saw Casey along with Harriet Edwards, who was carrying a large plate of cookies.

"Welcome, Mrs. Edwards," I said, getting to my feet. "Please come in."

Hardy stood as well. "Good afternoon, ma'am," he said cordially.

"I hope I am not intruding," Mrs. Edwards asked.

"Not at all," Hardy and I said together.

Hardy offered her his seat and moved over to the one next to it, so she would not have to walk any further.

Mrs. Edwards walked first over to me and placed the plate of coconut chocolate chip cookies on my desk.

"Here is your fee, Mr. Phelan," she announced triumphantly. "Paid in full."

"Yes, ma'am," I agreed, picking up one of the cookies and tasting it. It was just as delicious as I remembered.

Though I really did not want to share my treasure, I remembered my manners and offered them. Hardy and Casey each helped themselves.

"Mmmm," Casey said upon biting. "We need to do more legal work for her."

"Mrs. Edwards, would you care for one?" I asked.

"I'm not supposed to," she replied. "I have to watch my sugar, you know."

Then she seemed to think about it for a moment. "Oh, what the heck," she announced with a slight giggle. "At my age, I'm entitled."

We all laughed and ate more cookies. They were so good that the bruise on my face I had gotten for them seemed unimportant.

A small price to pay, I thought.

We were talking and having a nice time when the phone on Casey's desk started ringing.

"Would you excuse me, Mrs. Edwards?" Casey said, before heading off to her desk.

"Of course, dear," Edwards replied.

I could tell by the tone of Casey's voice that she was not at all pleased with whoever had called. A second later, my intercom buzzed. I picked up the phone receiver so only I could hear.

"Yes, Casey?"

"It's Old Iron Girdle on line one," she said testily. "She's demanding to speak to you about the judge's case."

I had no desire to speak with her, but felt I better take the call. I tapped the button for line one.

"Hello?"

"Mr. Phelan," Bollenbacher said sternly. "You left the courthouse before I could speak with you. I have some questions for you."

"This isn't exactly the best time right now —"

"It never is," she interrupted forcefully. "I paid for your services and I want answers."

"Fine," I replied. "I have time for two questions. No more."

"Good," she continued, "I want to know—"

"However," I interjected, "I reserve the right to not answer a question if I feel it violates my actual client's right to confidentiality. Are we clear?"

"We are," she answered. "Now, there was very little evidence brought forth at today's hearing."

"That's true," I responded.

"You told me that they have a video of the actual murder?"

"Not exactly," I said. "They have a video of the old pick-up truck that brought Russell to the site of his hanging. The killer was not seen."

"You said before that they could not get the license plate, right?"

"That's right, Miss Bollenbacher," I said, "and that's your second question."

"Wait a moment," she said, her voice rising in annoyance. "I was just confirming what you already told me."

"I've answered two questions, and I have to go now," I said.

"Just one more question," she insisted.

"Ma'am, we have been over this before," I said. "It is limited how much I can say about the case. You are not my client."

"I fail to understand why you cannot answer a simple question," Bollenbacher roared, finally losing her temper. "All I want to know is if the police have been able to identify the Ford pick-up truck!"

Her question troubled me, but I wasn't sure why. It was like a word on the tip of my tongue or a thought just beyond my memory. It was there, but I could not quite reach it.

"No, ma'am," I answered finally. "They have not."

I mumbled, "Goodbye," and hung up the phone. I sat for a moment hoping my brain could figure out exactly what was bothering me.

CHAPTER TWENTY-SEVEN

"Was that Ethel Bollenbacher?" Mrs. Edwards asked, breaking me out of my thoughts.

"Yes, it was." I answered.

"Oh, I wish I could have said hello," Edwards said in a disappointed voice. "I haven't seen her since poor Aggie died."

"Aggie?" I asked. "You mean Agnes Lawson?"

"Oh, yes," she said. "Aggie, Ethel, Dorothy Howard and I used to play mahjong every week for over thirty years. We used to call it our ladies' club."

"I remember Aggie talking about that," Hardy offered. "She would never miss it. Every Wednesday evening. She canceled a date with me once rather than miss her game."

"She loved to play," Edwards continued. "She and Ethel were the two best players. After all, they had been playing together since they were practically babies."

"How did they know each other?" I asked.

"Well, their fathers both owned horse farms and were the best of friends," she replied. "Ethel and Aggie were the closest friends I have ever seen. They were like sisters. When poor

Aggie died, we were all heartbroken, but Ethel was inconsolable."

I was dumbstruck. I guess focusing my mind on this new information was exactly what I needed because all at once I knew exactly why Ethel Bollenbacher's question bothered me so much. Now, everything made sense.

"Mrs. Edwards," I asked. "When you played together, did Aggie or Ethel ever talk about the death of Jill Lawson?"

A tear trickled down Mrs. Edwards' face when she heard my question. "Aggie never got over that. She was worried sick when her Jillie went missing. She still played, but we talked more about that case than anything else."

"What about after they found her?"

"It took the life right out of her," Edwards said. "She was so distraught, she actually missed a few games. Aggie and Ethel had never missed a game before. You can still play with only three, but it doesn't work as well."

"Did Aggie come back?"

"Yes, she did," Edwards said, "but she had changed."

"What do you mean?"

"Well, by then, they had arrested that awful man for killing Jillie," she said. "Aggie was so angry. She had always been such a kind soul, but losing her granddaughter was too much. She talked about nothing else. She told us all about the trial and the evidence. I remember the day after they convicted that horrible man, Aggie was saying such terrible and hateful things."

"What kind of things?" I pressed.

"She said that Russell deserved to die, but since there's no death penalty in New York, he would just go to prison," Edwards said, clearly uncomfortable with her memories. "Then she said ... well... "

"What did she say?" I asked.

"Well, she said some terrible things, but it wasn't really her.

Aggie was a wonderful woman, but she couldn't get over Jillie's death. You need to understand that," Edwards stressed. "What she said really wasn't who she was."

"I understand that," I said sympathetically, "but, it's important."

"She talked about things that she said happen to child killers in prison," Edwards said coldly. "I will not repeat them, but she hoped that every single disgusting one of them would happen to her granddaughter's killer."

"You don't have to repeat them," I said reassuringly.

"I won't," she insisted. "I hope you won't think badly of poor Aggie. She was never the same after Jillie was killed. It haunted her until the day she died. All of us always thought that when that monster killed little Jillie, he killed Aggie too. It just took longer for her to die."

Mrs. Edwards started to cry more freely now. Hardy grabbed a box of tissues off my desk and handed it to her.

"Thank you, John," she said through her tears.

I waited to let her regain her composure. I hated to force her to reveal more, but I had no choice.

"Mrs. Edwards, how did Ethel Bollenbacher react when Aggie passed?"

"As you would expect," she said. "She was crushed. Ethel never married. We three were the only people she was close with, and Aggie and she were even closer. Then, when that horrible man got released..."

"What happened?" I pushed.

"We stopped playing mahjong after Aggie died, but Dorothy and I would still get together, have lunch, and chat," Mrs. Edwards said. "We haven't seen Ethel since the funeral. We called her and asked us to join us, but she always refused."

"When was the last time you spoke to Ethel?" I asked.

"Oh, how could I ever forget that?" she replied. "It was the day that darn court ruled that Russell could go free. I called Ethel to see if she had heard. I figured working for a judge, she would know."

"What did she say?"

"She was so terribly upset," Edwards said, the tears resuming. "She sounded just like Aggie, saying all the dreadful things that should happen to that man... that monster. Please don't ask me to repeat them."

"You don't have to, Mrs. Edwards," I said, feeling terrible that I had forced out such painful memories.

"Mahjong was always an evening of fun for us," Mrs. Edwards said, standing up. "That evil man took it away. He killed Jillie and Agnes, and he poisoned such wonderful memories. God forgive me, but I am not sorry he's dead."

I called Casey into my office and asked her to drive Mrs. Edwards home. I thought Harriet Edwards might fight me on my request, being such an independent person. She did not.

Hardy offered to go along. This way, they could take Edwards' car and Casey's car, and have a way back to the office.

As soon as they were gone, I picked up the phone and called Ethel Bollenbacher. I started talking as soon she picked up.

"Miss Bollenbacher, this is Connor Phelan."

"Called me back so you can hang up on me, again?" she asked sarcastically.

"No," I replied. "If you would meet me at Judge Hardy's office, we can discuss the case in detail."

"About time," she answered before hesitating. "What changed your mind?"

"Not important," I said. "I'll meet you there in fifteen minutes."

"I'll be there," she said, and hung up the phone.

I scribbled a quick note for Casey and left. I hopped into my car and took off for the county courthouse. *It seems appropriate,* I thought, *for this case to end there.*

I parked in the courthouse lot and went inside. The judge's chambers were not locked. I went in and sat down in the judge's oversized chair. I found it very comfortable and thought that maybe someday down the road it might be nice to be a judge.

A few minutes later, the door opened and Ethel Bollenbacher walked in. She said nothing and just stared at me.

"Fancy yourself a judge?" she asked.

"Something like that," I said. "Please have a seat."

She sat in one of the attorney chairs in front of the desk.

"I've spent the last few days working on solving the murder of Gilbert Russell and the answer has been right in front of me all along," I said.

The blank stare of Ethel Bollenbacher never changed.

"What are you talking about?" she finally asked.

"Ever since I proved that John Hardy was innocent, I've been racking my brain trying to figure out who had a motive to kill Gilbert Russell," I said, watching her carefully.

"Everyone in the county hated that man," she answered.

"True," I conceded, "but just because drunks in the local bars talked about the kind of death he deserved and even boasted about wanting to kill him, doesn't make them real suspects. People love to talk about what child killers deserve, but very few plan to actually do it. It's just talk."

She said nothing and did not change her expression. So, I kept talking.

"I considered Al and Jamie Lawson," I said. "They wanted Russell dead and had good reason. If not them, then perhaps someone close to them who wanted to avenge their daughter."

"That would be a lot of people," Ethel added.

"Maybe," I agreed, "but that was not the killer's motive at all."

"Then, what was?" she asked.

"It was to avenge Aggie Lawson," I said, "and you know that."

"Aggie had many friends," she replied, her voice breaking slightly.

"But none closer than you," I insisted.

Ethel said nothing, but her eyes were glistening.

Not wanting to lose momentum, I pushed on.

"When Jill Lawson was murdered, it destroyed her grandmother, Aggie. She was never the same after that. Even when Gilbert Russell was captured and convicted, it still tore her apart. She died later of a heart attack, but everyone knew..."

"It was not a heart attack," Bollenbacher said quietly. "She was murdered by Gilbert Russell, just as surely as if he strangled her like he did to Jillie."

"Just as Jill's death destroyed Aggie," I pressed, "it was Aggie's suffering and death that tore you apart."

"A lot of us were upset when Aggie died, Mr. Phelan."

"Not like you were," I interrupted. "She was more than a friend to you. She was like a sister. You grew up together. You played at each other's horse farm. You did everything together until—"

"That ungodly monster killed her," she growled, finishing my sentence.

"Then, he got out of jail due to a legal error," I said, "and—"

"Legal error?" she laughed. "You mean because of the inept imbecile Worthington."

"Yes," I agreed, "that imbecile's stupid mistake let the murderer of Jill and Aggie go free."

I stopped talking and stared at Ethel for a moment. I could see the torment in her eyes as she was reliving the events of the past and feeling the personal agony. She was trying through sheer force of will not to break down, but the strain was evident.

"Someone had to make Gilbert Russell pay," I continued, putting more emotion in my voice to add to her strain. "He had to pay for his two murders."

I paused for a second before continuing to let my words seep in.

"Judge Hardy knew Aggie well. They had dated. That's why he lost his composure during sentencing and blurted out that Russell should have been taken out and hanged in the town square."

"He deserved such a fate," Ethel said, her anger barely contained.

"He did," I agreed. "So, when he got out, you made sure he paid for his crimes. You gave him a snap judgment and executed him."

"You can't prove that," she said through gritted teeth.

"Ah, but I can," I asserted. "Here's what I think happened. You waited outside The Rusty Bull while Russell was drinking inside. When he finally came out, you offered him a ride in the back tailgate. As he was climbing into the back of the truck, you put the truck in reverse and stomped on the accelerator. This made a big cloud of dust and made Russell fall into the back of the window."

"Utter fantasy, Mr. Phelan," Bollenbacher interrupted.

"Wait, there's more," I insisted. "The bartender didn't see you clearly, but he did say that after slamming the truck in reverse, the driver waited twenty or thirty seconds before taking off."

"So?" she asked.

"The autopsy report showed that Gilbert Russell died both from strangulation from being hanged and an overdose of Ketamine, a horse tranquilizer. You grew up on a horse farm, as did Aggie. You knew how to tranquilize a horse and had access to Ketamine and a tranq gun."

She said nothing, so I continued. "I figure you jammed the truck into reverse to make him fall into the back window of the truck. Then, you took the twenty to thirty seconds to open the back window and shoot Russell in the ass with a tranq dart. This way, he would not able to fight you when you hanged him. Then you drove into town square which was deserted to the tree where you had probably already tied the rope. You pinned the note to this shirt, tied the other end of the rope around his neck, got back in the truck, and pulled away. Russell was yanked back by the rope and hanged."

"A fascinating story, but as I said before, you can't prove it," she said acerbically.

"As I said before, Miss Bollenbacher," I said back in the same tone, "I can."

"There's one more thing the killer needed to do all of this that eliminates almost all other suspects," I said.

Ethel took a deep breath before speaking. "And what is that, Mr. Phelan."

"The killer also had access to Aggie's truck."

I noticed Ethel slightly raise her eyebrows when I mentioned the truck.

"Yes, Aggie's truck," I pressed. "As you know, that was the truck used to bring Gilbert Russell to the tree where he was hanged."

"I didn't know that until you just told me, Mr. Phelan," she insisted.

"Yes, you did," I responded. "You proved that when you spoke to me on the phone today."

"And how did I do that?" she said, her anger beginning to show.

"You said and I quote, 'All I want to know is if the police have been able to identify the Ford pick-up truck!'"

"You told me about the truck prior to that," she insisted.

"Yes, I did. But I only said it was an old pick-up truck. I never told you it was a Ford. The police, district attorney, Dom Bryce, and I—we all knew that the truck used in the murder was a Ford," I said. "It was never made public. You knew because you are the only other person who could know—the killer."

She hung her head and began to cry. I grabbed a box of tissues and slid it across the desk to her.

"I already have what I need," she answered. Her head came up and in her hand was a small Derringer two-shot pistol, pointed right at my chest.

CHAPTER TWENTY-EIGHT

"You are a very arrogant and infuriating man," Ethel lamented. "You wouldn't answer a simple question and got me so angry that I—"

"Said something stupid," I finished.

"Yes, stupid," she agreed.

"I thought you kept calling out of concern for the judge," I said. "I figured that after all these years you were in love with him. Turns out, you were just trying to see if anyone was on to you."

"I do love John Hardy," she said, "but not romantically. I felt terrible when he was arrested. What I don't understand is how his hair got to the scene."

"It was planted," came a voice from across the room.

Ethel spun around and saw John Hardy standing in the doorway.

"Worthington had Officer Brubaker set me up so the local politicos wouldn't nominate me for re-election in March."

"John," Ethel said in surprise. "How did you know we were even here?"

"Connor called me from his car," he said, letting the cat out of the bag. "He told me it was you. I came over to hear it for myself."

Ethel stared at him silently for a long time.

"Connor didn't tell me why," Hardy continued.

"You want to know why?" Ethel roared. "I'll tell you. That son of a bitch killed Jillie and killed Aggie as sure as if he put a gun in her mouth and pulled the trigger."

She took a deep breath and choked back her tears.

"It was just as you said, Mr. Phelan," she continued, without looking at me. "I took Aggie's truck. I knew where the keys were and had driven it many times. Aggie had bad arthritis in her hands and sometimes asked me to drive for her."

She sniffed loudly before continuing. "I parked outside the gin mill where that lowlife was drinking and toasting his freedom. You heard what he said in court, John. He was ready to get more *girlfriends*. He was bragging about raping and killing more innocent little children. That horrible beast had to be stopped. So, when he came out, he was so drunk, he could barely walk. I offered him a ride home. He climbed in and... well... the rest you know."

"One thing I'm not certain about," I said. "What was the point of the fancy note? Was it to formally announce Russell's execution to the world?"

Ethel smiled sadly before responding.

"That's between Aggie and me."

Tears began streaming down her face as emotions she had been trying to keep buried finally surfaced.

"She was my sister, John," she blurted through sobs, "and Jillie was my granddaughter too. Maybe not by blood, but they were!

That monster took them from me," she sobbed. "He

molested and strangled Jillie, and killed Aggie over time through heartbreak, sorrow, and depression. He took everything from me in this world that I loved. Now, I'm all alone."

She whirled back to me and raised her gun.

"I've got no problem killing you, Mr. Phelan," she said, before turning back to Judge Hardy. "But I don't want to kill you, John. At our age, we don't have many close friends left."

Hardy stepped forward and held out his hand.

"Give me the gun, Ethel," he said quietly.

For a few tense seconds, she just stared at him. Then her hand started to tremble in rhythm with her crying. Finally, she handed the Derringer to Hardy who put it in his jacket pocket.

Ethel's sobs began to grow as the last vestiges of control evaporated. Hardy reached out and pulled her into an embrace. Ethel began to openly weep as she grieved the end of everything in her life she had held dear. After a few minutes, the sound diminished, though she still cried on Hardy's shoulder.

I heard the outer door open and seconds later Bills and one of the court officers came into the room with Worthington right behind them. Right after I called John Hardy from my car, I had called Bills to make sure he would be here. I had also told him why. I assumed he had invited Worthington. I was glad he had.

I assumed they must have heard Ethel's wailing. They observed the room for a moment, but said nothing.

"Bills," I said softly, "Miss Bollenbacher just confessed to the murder of Gilbert Russell. She needs to be taken into custody."

Ethel pulled away from Judge Hardy. She raised her hand to his cheek and caressed it softly.

"I am sorry, John," she said softly, "I never intended for you to get in trouble."

"I know, Ethel," he replied. "I know."

Ethel walked quietly over to Bills and held out her hands.

"I am ready, Mr. Billingsley," she said.

"Now, just a moment," Worthington piped up, "I decide who gets arrested in this county."

Before I could say a word, Ethel walked stridently over to Worthington.

"Be quiet, you imbecile," she said defiantly, and slapped him hard across the face.

Worthington took a step back, stunned from the slap. He seemed confused for a second before he regained his composure.

"Well, don't just stand there, officer," Worthington bellowed. "Arrest that woman."

Ethel put out her hands and waited for the handcuffs. Bills just smiled.

"That's all right, Miss Bollenbacher," he said kindly. "Just go with Officer Kennedy please."

Kennedy escorted her out.

"Can you believe the nerve of that woman?" Worthington shouted. "She struck me."

"The way I see it," I offered. "You had it coming."

"I beg your pardon," the district attorney sneered.

"You made a deal with Officer Brubaker," I asserted. "In return for planting evidence against John Hardy, you offered him the position of Chief Investigator."

"Rubbish," Worthington roared. "You can't prove a word of it."

"No, I can't," I admitted. "You put Brubaker on a plane to Chicago. Without him, there's no proof."

Worthington smiled triumphantly.

"However," I said loudly, causing Worthington's smile to drop like a sack of potatoes, "Dom Bryce is searching for him. When he finds him, I'm sure he'll get a written statement from him admitting the whole thing."

"Then it will be his word against mine, won't it?" Worthington sneered. "Who do you think the public will believe? A cop on the run or the duly elected district attorney?"

"On the run?" I asked. "Your office declined to prosecute him. Don't you remember?"

"Those charges could be reinstated," he said defensively.

"I see," I said in a mocking tone. "So, when you arraign him on those exact same charges, what will you say to Judge Marino when he arraigns him? Are you going to admit to *Judge Marino* that you lied to his face? After all, he is such a patient man."

Worthington grunted loudly in frustration and started for the door. Hardy grabbed him by the arm and pulled him back.

"What is this?" the district attorney demanded. "Let go of me, John!"

"John?" Hardy said loudly. "You are in my chambers, counsel."

"Excuse me," Worthington said in a snotty tone, "Let go of me *Your Honor*.

"That's better," Hardy replied. "Now, in light of everything I have been through this past week, I have something for you."

"What's that?" Worthington asked.

"This," Hardy said, before belting the district attorney square in the mouth.

Worthington fell backwards and landed flat on his back. A black hole appeared where there once had been two of his front teeth and blood trickled down his mouth."

"That's assault," Worthington shouted through the remnants of his teeth. "You're going to jail.

"Your honor," I interjected. "If I were you, I would quote exactly what District Attorney Worthington said to me this very day outside of Judge Marino's chambers."

"And what would that be?" Hardy asked.

I looked down at Worthington as I said, "Even if it were true, you can't prove it."

"Officer Billingsley," Worthington shouted. "You saw it. Arrest Hardy, and arrest Phelan as his accomplice!"

Bills initially said nothing. He walked over to Worthington and helped him to his feet. It took little effort to do so since Bills was such a bear of a man.

"Don't just stand there, officer!" the district attorney shouted.

"Just a moment," Bills said softly.

Bills reached into his jacket pocket and pulled out a white envelope.

"This is for you, sir," he said to Worthington, placing it in his hand.

"What's this?" Worthington demanded.

"That is my resignation," Bills replied. "Earlier today, I put in my retirement papers."

"I don't care about that," the district attorney snapped. "Just arrest them."

"I'm retired," Bills said. 'I can't arrest anybody."

"What is going on here?" Worthington demanded.

"You had Brubaker frame Judge Hardy and promised him my job in return," Bills said angrily. "There's no room in the budget for both of us. That means you were going to fire me."

"But, but..." Worthington stammered.

"But nothing," Bills insisted, his voice terrifying. "After all my years of service, this is how you treat me?"

Worthington's eyes went wide with panic.

"You know what I ought to do?" Bills asked.

He then took his mammoth fist and put it up to Worthington's face. His fist was nearly as large as the district attorney's entire head.

Worthington's face went white as a ghost and he fainted out of sheer terror.

I hated to see Bills retire, but I understood why. He was all about respect and honor. The actions of the district attorney were too much for him to bear. I would miss him.

A few seconds later, a familiar odor came wafting up from Worthington's prone body telling us all that he had soiled himself. As the three of us headed for the door, Judge Hardy groaned.

"What's the matter?" I asked.

"Now, I'm going to have to have that carpet changed."

After Bills carried Worthington back to his office, the three of us left the building and agreed to go straight to The Cardinal. We had to celebrate John Hardy being exonerated and Roger Billingsley's retirement. It wasn't far and we planned on drinking. So, we decided to walk.

I pulled out my cell phone and called Dom and invited him to join us. I then called the office and invited Casey. After I assured her that I would pay her for the full day even if we shut down now, she agreed to join us.

I couldn't reach Becky. I knew she had to work tonight, so she would be unavailable. I was sorry about that. I wanted very much to share this victory with her. In my heart, I knew I wanted to share everything with her.

The words of Ethel Bollenbacher had hit me hard.

He took everything from me in this world that I loved. Now, I'm all alone.

I had felt like that after my wife and unborn child died. Everything I loved had vanished. I was alone. That feeling had lasted until Becky came back in my life. She had given me a happiness I never thought I would experience again. I had no intention of losing that feeling.

As we continued to walk, I also remembered Mr. Ito's words as he left my house the night before.

Don't let this one get away, Connor. She's something special.

I used my phone to do a quick Google search. Hoping neither Hardy nor Billingsley would notice, I went to the web site for a local jewelry store and started looking at diamond engagement rings.

THE END

A NOTE FROM THE PUBLISHER

Thank you for reading this book. If you enjoyed it please do consider leaving a review on Amazon to help others find it too.

We hate typos. All of our books have been rigorously edited and proofread, but sometimes mistakes do slip through. If you have spotted a typo, please do let us know and we can get it amended within hours.

info@bloodhoundbooks.com